CATCHING CALLIE

CLAIRE WOODS

BLURB

GABE

The Press calls me campuses "DIRTY PLAYER.

The scandal I got trapped in just made the national news, ESPN, & Sports Illustrated.

Forced to hide out in a small beach town until I can clear my name, the last thing I expected was to run into her.

Literally.

But she wants nothing to do with me.

Even my killer smile and panty-melting grin didn't work.

She ran.

Twice.

But I have six weeks to find my mystery girl, get my reputation back, and prove to her I'm not a dirty player: I'm her prince, and the football field is the domain I rule, and her heart is the next thing I'm going to win.

GAME ON.

ONE

GABE

"GABE! OVER HERE! Is it true? Does the University have a different set of academic standards for athletes?"

"GABE! Did you cheat?"

"Are you on academic probation?"

Camera's flash—blinding me as dozens of reporters box me in, shoving microphones in my face. I can't even throw up the hood of my sweatshirt since I'm too busy swatting them away.

What in the hell is going on?

My hands hastily swipe my coded key card to enter the sports complex. I'm forced to push them firmly back, snapping the door shut. All they can do now is shout through the thick glass.

That was a friggin' bloodbath.

Rounding the hall to the offices, I suddenly feel like a kid going to detention.

"Coach? You wanted to see me?"

He's pissed. His face red all the way to his receding hairline.

"Can you explain this?"

He swivels his computer screen around.

Shit.

A picture of me in my football uniform is at the center of the page under a headline:

DIRTY PLAYER!

Star Running Back, GABE PARKER at the center of University cheating scandal. According to several sources close to him, "academics aren't the only thing he cheats at."

"There must be a mistake."

"It's not a mistake," Coach replies through thin lips, eyes glaring hard at *me*: his star player and best shot of making the playoffs this year. He slides some papers across his desk.

A trickle of sweat falls down the back of my neck. *How in the fuck did this happen?* Staring at the exam in my hand with red ink penned all over it—the pit in my stomach grows.

"This is bullshit. I didn't cheat," I roar, pounding my fist on his desk.

He turns his monitor back around. "That was just the local paper... others are worse."

"What are we going to do?"

Coach sits back in his chair causing it to squeak, puts his hands behind his head and replies, "Not us. YOU. Here." He picks up a brochure flinging it at me, "you've already been enrolled for the first summer session at the satellite campus in Sea Spray."

"Sea Spray? Never heard of it."

Coach leans forward coming off his chair, bracing his

weight on his forearms, "don't fuck this up, Parker. The team needs you. You have five weeks to re-take those exams in question, pass your summer classes and get your ass in gear for preseason. There can't even be a shred of doubt that you cheated last semester. I talked the dick off of a bull to keep you from getting expelled."

"Expelled? I didn't do *shit*."

"I know that, son. But the NCAA's been on our asses ever since that exposé was published in Sports Illustrated claiming our athletes maintain their grades through scamming the system—walking out on graduation days with GPA's they didn't earn."

Shaking my head, I bend forward, running a hand nervously down my thigh. *"That is fucking bullshit."*

"Maybe. But the fact is you passed the first exam perfectly and when they retested you with a different one you bombed."

"Fucking Jackie," I mutter under my breath.

"What's that?"

"Nothing, Sir. Forget it."

A knock at the door interrupts what he was going to say. "Coach?"

"What is it, Jimmy?"

"The press is here. News trucks from all the big networks, too. Sports Illustrated, and ESPN just broke the story—it got picked up nationally. They want blood."

"Fuck." We both mutter at the same time.

Coach opens his desk, taking out a key.

"What's this?"

"Salvation. Don't screw it up."

"Coach?"

"It's a house key. To a house in Sea Spray on the beach that belonged to my Nan. You can hide out there, keep your head down and your dick in your pants, and let this shit blow over until the next big sports story breaks."

The metal key feels warm in my palm. My throat closes. Coach knows I can't go home. I planned to stay in one of the dorms for free this summer in exchange for working a few shifts a week at the student health club.

"You can go out through the tunnel. I'll have Jimmy pick you up and drive you back to the dorms. Classes start again in two weeks. Keep your head down, Gabe. You have the potential to go pro. The future is in the palm of your hand, kid."

Getting up to leave, I hesitate, looking back. "I want you to know, that I didn't cheat. My ex, Jackie showed up at the team's house off-campus out of her mind. She accused me of hooking up with someone else and all sorts of shit. I-we broke up, and the exam re-take was the next morning. My head wasn't right. I was tired as hell. I'm sorry, Coach. I just wanted you to know you didn't go to bat for a cheater."

He nods his head. "I'll check in with you. Oh, before I forget... the University picked up the tab for your summer classes, but I assume you still need a job?"

My hand on the door, I turn around nodding my head.

"When you get into town, stop by the satellite campus security office. I got you one."

"Me? Working security?"

"What? Be grateful. It'll buy you gas and food."

"Thanks, Coach." My hand jerks the door open. I pull my hoodie up over my face. But it's not like my six-foot-three frame with shoulders as broad as a bus can melt into the walls. My flip flops clap as I walk hurriedly through the maze of halls and offices underneath the campus sports complex.

My cell buzzes in my left hand.

Fucking Jackie again.

She knows I stay here, at UVA during breaks and she managed to get an internship as a paralegal nearby to be close.

Ignoring her call, I open the heavy door leading to the tunnel. The tunnel travels the whole length of the football field underground. It'll dump me out on the other side at the parking lot.

Hopefully, there are no reporters there. Maybe, spending the summer away from here will do me good. I'll get away from Jackie, focus on my fitness routine, and come back at the top of my game, literally.

"Fuck." I stare at my phone in disbelief. There's no cell service in the tunnel but my long legs cross it in under five minutes. My phone is lighting the eff up, fifty texts, dozens of missed calls. And a number I dread more than Jackie's—my father's.

"Get in," Jimmy roars, opening the passenger door to his old pick-up. I don't need another invitation as news trucks and camera's line the other side of the field.

"I've got bad news."

"Oh, yeah? What could be worse?" I mutter, trying to stretch my hood even tighter over my face.

"They're camped out by both entrances to your dorm. Give me your key-card. Some of the boys on the team are meeting to clear out your shit. Get in your car and drive straight to Sea Spray."

"Fuck," I mutter. In less than one hour, my life has become a damn circus. I don't know how celebrities hack it.

Jimmy drops me off at my old Ford Explorer. I have a full tank of gas and nothing but the clothes on my back. Feeling like a fugitive, I whip my sunglasses on peeling out while checking my rearview.

My Bluetooth connects... muttering a string of curses so foul the devil would blush, I call him back.

"DIRTY PLAYER?"

"Cee Cee is going ballistic," he roars.

"Get your ass back home now!"

"Gee, thanks for asking how I'm doing, *Dad*."

"Fuck, Gabe. You will drop off the team, and transfer to NYU for your senior year. I've already made the calls and a generous donation."

"No thanks. I can handle this myself."

"The hell you can! It's a goddamn humiliation. My son? The Dirty Player? Cheating on and off the field? It's an embarrassment to me as well. I'm a federal judge. Your behavior is reflecting poorly on me."

"Funny, I've had a girlfriend for the past two years."

"As if that ever stops anyone."

"You must be talking about yourself. But I'm nothing like you *DAD*. You think I give a shit that, that chick you married who is only ten years older than me is embarrassed? Get a clue, Dad. I'm not coming home. The last time I did, your precious Cee Cee tried to fuck me."

"That's it. You're dead to me. Don't come calling for money."

"As if I ever did," I reply disconnecting.

"Fuck!" Pounding my fists against the steering wheel, my jaw clenches. No one ever believes in me. They see me as the star athlete, king of campus, and as a womanizer. But who I am —is just a guy wishing his life wasn't so fucked up.

TWO

GABE

THE DRIVE TOOK TWO HOURS. The pit in my stomach and acid burning the back of my throat didn't ease up. But then I reached Sea Spray—a tiny nothing of a town outside Virginia Beach.

I shut off my AC and opened the windows. It's been years since I smelled the tangy salt of the ocean.

Cranking up the music, I sing out loud with Tom Petty. I'm free falling myself, but somehow at this moment rolling into town, it feels like everything is going to be all right.

"Yeah, I'm free—" I belt out not caring everyone stopped at the traffic light are gaping while some laugh... others honk.

Feeling great, like I do at the end of a big game where I crush it—my foot hits the gas just as the light turns. My eyes close for a second, I'm killing the last verse.

My car hits something.

Honks followed by screams make me stomp on the breaks hard. My seat belt locks; slamming the car into park I jump out afraid of what I'm going to find.

She's trembling. Her bike's caught under the front of my car; both her knees are scraped and bloody.

"Holy Shit! I didn't see you."

"I was in the crosswalk."

"The light was green."

"Oh yeah, well the cross signal was green for me when I started."

"Christ," I mutter, walking forward. "Are you okay?"

She's mute, looking down.

"I'll buy you a new bike. Hell, I'll drive you to the hospital if you want. Please—can we leave the cops out of this?"

She crosses her arms eyes shooting daggers, "you almost killed me."

"Yeah, I know," my hand rubs the back of my neck, "but I didn't."

She stares at me stunned. "Only because I jumped off my bike when it was clear you were having an American Idol moment."

My lips twitch. "I've had a real shit day. Can I at least buy you a drink?"

The rest of the onlookers start to leave when it's clear she's okay.

"No thanks," she mutters grabbing the mangled handlebars attempting to jerk her bike free.

"Let me."

"No." She hip-checks me but ends up falling on her ass instead.

"Sweetheart, I insist," my eyes roll.

"Did you just roll your eyes at me?"

"I did."

"I changed my mind. I'm calling this in."

Her hands reach inside her fanny pack for her phone. Before her fingers slippery from sweat and nerves get it, I grab it, clutching it to my chest like a prized toy on Christmas morning.

She blows a wisp of hair from her eyes. "No, you didn't."

"I did."

She shakes her head. "I was willing to let this go if you paid for a new bike since it's clear you can't make a living with that nineties boy band voice of yours—I'd hate for you to have to pay the fine for hitting a pedestrian."

"Pretty please?" I give her my best panty-melting grin that shows my dimples.

She huffs, crossing her arms over her chest, the motion squishing her breasts together; her cleavage now pops over her sports tank top.

It can't be helped.

It's bred in my male DNA to drop my gaze.

"Figures." She taps her foot pissed I'm acting like a pig.

"Right. Let me back up my SUV to free your bike, and we can exchange information."

"Sure," she grumbles with a quick wave of her hand.

"Don't be so grumpy, fanny pack. You'd be cute otherwise."

"Fanny pack?'"

"Yup. I haven't seen one of those since my Mom's picture album labeled 1983."

"Jerk."

Grinning for the first time in days, I turn on my heel putting my car in reverse. I don't use the backup camera, worried I could still hit something else. Slowly backing up a few feet, one arm draped behind the headrest of my empty passenger seat, I safely brake then put the car back in park.

"See. I'm actually a safe driver," I call out opening the door.

But she's gone.

Vanished.

The blinking yellow hazard lights reflect off the twisted metal laying in a heap.

"Well, shit. I did almost kill her," I mutter to the fireflies coming out to play in the twilight. Which would've been a complete shame, since she seemed to be in a select club of women who don't seem to have a clue—who I am.

"And that's the story of how my shitty day ended," I tell my buddy, Trey.

"Jesus, Gabe."

"I know."

"Well, how is Coach's Gran's house? You got pink toilet rugs and crochet doilies everywhere?"

My eyes flit over the cozy cottage with whitewashed walls, wicker furniture, and a fair selection of hand knit doilies on end tables with old-fashioned lamps on them. The kind where there's a wick dipped in oil with a lighter placed nearby.

"Yup."

"Sounds like paradise."

"Actually, it is." My feet cross the wide plank floors to the sliding French doors opened wide letting the wind whip through bringing fresh ocean air inside.

The moon hangs low, its light guiding the waves straight to my back door like a beacon. The combination of the full moon and high tide bringing the crashing waves feet from breaking in front of my bare feet.

"I might not come back."

"You're shittin' me, right?"

"Yeah. But man, this place is just what I need right now."

"Especially since, old pictures of us are blowing up Instagram, MeWow, and Tinder."

"Shit. The ones from freshman year or last?"

"Both."

"Damn, this is worse than I thought."

"Well, it was your idea to pledge to Kappa Delta in addition to being on the football team. You said, and I remember at the time, 'in case going pro doesn't work out we can fall back on the brotherhood.'"

"Christ, I was half in the bag."

"Well, you need to put a bag over your head until this crap dies down."

"Yeah. That's probably not a bad idea."

Hanging up, I place my phone on Gran's teak table, whip off my hoodie and strip down to my boxer briefs. Jogging towards the breaking waves, I look left then right. Like I'm crossing traffic.

With a grin, I peel my boxers down, toss them onto the sand and dive straight in.

Surfacing, I float on my back, dick saluting the moon and make a wish on the brightest star on the opposite end of the horizon.

The first thing that pops into my head isn't wishing the shit storm in my life to go away.

*It's to find her—m*y fanny pack girl and get her name.

THREE

CALLIE

I DON'T KNOW WHY I DID IT—Just turned and walked away into the night, leaving him to deal with the pile of junk in the road.

He just pissed me the hell off, driving in like the boys of summer do in their fancy SUV's acting like they own our town.

Ever year they leave the same way they ride in—like bats out of hell.

I learned that lesson the hard way, the summer I turned eighteen when Elliot Langston III came here to spend the summer with his grandmother Elizabeth Canton Langston.

He held my hand telling me I was the most beautiful girl he'd ever seen. And like a young teenager trapped in first love—I hung on every honeyed word that fell from his lips.

Under the dancing seagrass and behind the dunes, I let him peel off my shorts, strip me of my panties and steal my virginity.

Despite the romantic setting—sand got in my ass and every fold between my thighs causing him to feel like sandpaper when he thrusted in.

It hurt like hell, was hardly arousing—I've never wanted to repeat the experience called sex again. The next time I saw him was a year later in the society page section of the Washington D.C. Journal. He's from some filthy rich, political family or something. They were at a fundraiser; ironically for the National Cancer Foundation.

No guy since Elliot has even made me look twice much less think about them in that way.

But American Idol singer—he was something else.

He was as tall as a superhero with shoulders just as wide. But superheroes don't run over girls—*they rescue them.*

His amber eyes sparkled when he realized I wasn't seriously hurt when he ribbed me for my fanny pack. But damn did I melt when he flashed me those panty melting dimples. That with his chiseled jaw and athletic body are going to break a lot of hearts at the shore this summer.

I just don't want mine to be one of them.

Sighing, I bend down slipping off my sneakers when I reach the sand. It's only the end of May. Memorial Day is next weekend. After that, the season will be in full swing. The streets will be full of traffic, the restaurants will be crowded, and the sand will be littered with babes in bikinis with summer boys eyeing every one.

I wanted to enjoy the solitude of the beach at night before the bonfires, beer bottles, and parties descend. My cell rings from inside my *fanny pack* disrupting my thoughts.

"Callie? Where are you?"

"Hey, Gina. I'm on the beach."

"The shop closes in five minutes."

"I know. Sorry I couldn't stop by. Some blockhead summer boy hit me in the crosswalk."

"WHAT? I'll kill him myself. You called your Uncle Steve, right? He'd thrown that asshole in jail, for sure."

My toes dig into the soft sand, "no. No, I didn't."

"Why the hell not? Are you okay? Did they call an ambulance?"

"Yes, I'm fine. No, there was no need for an ambulance. But —you are down one less bike to rent."

"That's fine sweetie, that's what insurance is for. Sleep in tomorrow and come in after lunch."

"Thanks, Gina."

My Aunt Gina's the best. She and Uncle Steve are my Dad's siblings. Gina's closer to me than them since she was born fifteen years after them. She's who Gran would refer to as her, "Oops, baby."

I never knew what that meant until sex-ed class.

Now, I know more about the human body than most. I'm studying to be a physician. I want to help sick people get better. It's something I've always wanted. Getting accepted into Virginia's elite State University was easy. But I had no choice but to defer a year to stay here, help Dad run the shops, look after Charlie, and hold Mom's hand as she went through her treatments.

I don't regret one second of it.

Only she didn't respond to the chemo the way we hoped. The doctors added stem cell therapy, but instead of deferring again I started taking classes at the new satellite campus that opened up last summer.

It's as if God saw my struggles and cleared up a path for me. I breathe in the humid summer air with a sigh of relief. The mile-long walk on the beach went fast.

What the heck?

I almost trip on a pile of clothes. Pausing, I glance in all directions. There's no one else here. But out in the water under a beam of blinding moonlight, a dark head bobs.

"Crazy idiot. Sharks feed at night." I shake my head. Looking back down, I grin recognizing the gray hoodie.

It can't be.

Gingerly, I bend down, taking it in my hands.

It smells like him.

My breasts tingle; thighs ache.

With no one to see, I press it to my nose closing my eyes. The fragrance industry sure knows what they're about. My hormones are driving the bus, and I'm tempted to strip my clothes off and ride that pony swimming in the moonlight.

But I don't.

I have a better idea instead.

Snagging the rest of his clothing, I jog away from the surf towards the dunes covered in shadows.

"HEY!" He calls out swimming furiously towards shore.

But summer boy doesn't know these beach paths as I do. He doesn't stand a chance.

Especially naked.

But how could I know he's as fast as an Olympian?

He tackles me from behind—I fall, face-planting in the sand. His clothes acting as a barricade saves me from sand scrapes.

"What the hell?" He mutters, turning me over.

"Fanny pack?"

"Um... *hi*?"

"Well, this is interesting." He smiles down on me, elbows planted in the sand on either side of my body.

Oddly, I'm not afraid of being pinned down in the moonlight by this handsome stranger—until—it dawns on me he's naked as the day he was born. Something hard rocks into the cradle between my hips causing me to gasp as he shifts his weight.

"Sorry," he rolls to the side for a second giving me room to get up. "Fuck it. I'm not sorry." He rolls back on top of me, tracing a finger over my stunned, parted lips. "I made a wish on a star tonight. Haven't done that since I was ten. And here you are, showing up here like a thief in the moonlight. Technically, you are a thief. Maybe I should call the cops on you, baby?"

I can't answer. It's happening to me again, and I'm helpless to stop it.

I'm drowning on dry land, star gazing into his eyes as his head lowers a breath from mine. "Thank you for turning the shittiest day I ever had, into the best one," he murmurs capturing my lips.

Instinctually, my thighs open, womb wanting to cradle his hips and invite him inside.

"So sweet," he murmurs against my lips a second before his tongue boldly comes out to play with mine. "But you won't need this." With a smirk, he unclasps the buckle to my fanny pack tossing it next to my sneakers that dropped when he caught me. His lips never leave mine. He does this so smoothly and skillfully as if seduction is his profession.

Elliott never kissed me like this. Hell, I doubt even Jamie Dornan can kiss like this.

My hands clutch his head, nails raking through his hair as I hungrily kiss him back.

His hands come up under my shirt causing me to hiss when he touches the spot on my ribs where the pavement scraped.

He lowers his head to inspect the marks his hands feel.

"Did I cause this?"

My reply is a gasp as he trails a fire of kisses along my ribcage up to my breasts. He unclasps the front snap bra I put on, and my breasts spring free from confinement.

"Christ, you're beautiful," he moans, worshiping my breasts with his wet tongue, licking and sucking them.

He rolls back on his heels one arm around my back to lift

me closer to his hungry mouth. The large palm on his other hand presses my breasts together so that he can suck both nipples at the same time.

"Oh. My. God." My voice sounds crazy even to my ears.

I'm on fire. My clit's swollen, my body's primed and ready to go.

I feel his smile against my skin as he drops one hand, cupping my sex hard.

I nearly break my nose on his chin as my body jolts like it's been struck by a live wire.

"What is it?"

"Huh?" I'm lost at sea. Hungry, weak and entirely disoriented by his mad voodoo make out skills.

"You're name, cupcake."

My eyes lower. He's unashamed, almost proud of it as he catches me dropping my eyes.

It's beautiful.

I've never thought dicks were beautiful. Maybe I cracked my head on the concrete because his is a work of art.

"It fits."

"What?"

"My size. It's proportionate to my body."

My face flames. Am I really talking to the stranger who almost killed me about his dick size?

Shaking my head, I curse myself.

"Nope."

"What?"

"This is not happening," I gesture between the two of us.

"Why not?" He whispers looking... hurt?

"Because," I answer standing up and brushing the sand from my legs, " the last time I was out here with a naked guy behind the dunes it didn't end well."

"Did he hurt you?" His fists clench as he stands.

"Not that way... although, I can attest that having sex on sand is not as hot as you'd think."

He cocks an eyebrow, "Oh, fanny. We'd burn so hot—the ocean would catch fire."

He grabs his shorts and turns around. I bite my lip. His ass is just as fine as the rest of him. Every muscle is cut, lines delineating each part.

Before I can think, I swipe his shirt, grab my pack and take off,

"Why are you running again?" He laughs behind me. "I don't need to chase you when we have a habit of running into one another."

And honestly, I'm not running from him. I'm running from myself.

"Crap." A jagged shell cut through my underfoot. I left my sneakers. I took his shirt but left my shoes. In less than two hours I've lost my bike, my sanity and now my shoes to that... that—*dirty player*.

There's no doubt in my mind that's who he is. He reduced me to a puddle of mush, a woman not caring for anything but the need to have that man between her legs.

I don't like it. It's foreign. Alien. I've been so busy busting my ass that I forgot what it felt like to slow down and act like a woman out of adolescence. I don't get many chances to anyway. With Mom getting sick; leaving Dad and me to run the two family businesses we own.

My best friend Sophie's house is a couple of dunes over. Hobbling down the beach path, I feel like a complete mess. Horny, in pain, and in dire need of spilling to my best friend what just happened.

I don't bother knocking but head to the side of her house, following the smell of the smoke from the bonfire her dad usually has going.

"Callie? What the hell happened to you?" She bolts out of an Adirondack chair.

Chin quivering, feeling like a lost, hot mess, I try not to cry.

"Callie?"

"Some hot stranger hit me on the bike. Then he—we—made out by the dunes and he almost made me come."

"What?" Wine spews from her mouth. She takes me by the hand, leading me through the sliding glass doors inside and straight up to the small bathroom adjoining her room.

"Strip."

She turns the shower on and takes a fluffy towel from the shelf. "You're bleeding."

"Yeah, I ran out on him and forgot my shoes. But I grabbed this."

I hold up the gray T-shirt.

"He goes to UVA."

"Shit. I didn't bother looking at the emblem on his shirt when I was so busy sniffing it."

"Well lucky for you, you'll be at the same campus as your mystery man in a few months. Hey, don't cry. I know you don't have much experience with guys, it's normal to be horny and make out with strangers. In fact, that's what freshman year was mostly about."

"Yeah, well. That isn't me," I mutter stepping into the hot spray. The water stings as I lather soap over my cuts, cleaning them free of sand. I grit my teeth, shaking my head, at how easily a hot guy and his mega dick made me forget the world. Forget my own damn name.

FOUR

GABE

I ROLL OVER and groan. I had forgotten to close the blinds last night and the sun peaks over the horizon stretching its rays wide, straight through the window hitting the bed.

I slept like a rock after swimming in the cold ocean for forty-five minutes after she fled. My cock was as hard as dried concrete. I didn't feel like jerking off in Coach's Gran's house. So, I swam it off, half-thinking a shark was going to think it was a midnight snack.

The thought helped shrink me as I swam. But damn my mystery girl was... *fine.*

Her breasts were high and just full enough to fill my hands. I still remember the taste of her: sweet tea and chocolate.

Christ. My morning wood wants to go. It looks like I'm going to go swimming with the sharks again. My cell rings on the nightstand; my hand slaps out feeling for it.

"Rise and shine asshole!"

"Trey?"

"Yup. Marcus and I are on our way. We come bearing gifts.

We got all your crap out of the dorm yesterday. Damn, you are in some shit."

"Don't I know it."

"We'll be there by lunch. Oh, and Jackie showed up. She had her high heels pointed at my balls, threatening to stab them if I didn't tell her where you are.

I pinch the bridge of my nose closing my eyes. "You didn't."

"Hell no. But Marcus being the dumbass he did let it slip that you fled to the beach."

"Fucking Marcus. I'm going to kick the shit out of him."

"Yeah, well. There's more, bro... we all got caught in this mess. The University is opening an official investigation. Coach said we might need attorneys and shit. Maybe you could call your father?"

"Fuck no. I don't need any more crap from him. We'll figure this out on our own."

"Dude? He's a federal judge, and before that, he was the top prosecutor in Manhattan."

"I said no."

"Okay, but we need to get a handle on this. You and I have a shot to go pro. No team will want us if this sticks, due to the bad press it'll bring. It'll follow us around like a bad hook-up."

Ending the call, I fall back on the pillows, dick deflated. At least that's one less problem I have.

After a few minutes. I know what I need to do. I'm about to be a senior at one of the top University's in the country, playing on a premier football team with the chance to be drafted.

I'm not going down like this.

And I'm not going to depend on anyone else to clean up the mess I landed in.

Swiping my phone back open, I scroll through until I find the President of the University's number.

"Gabriel Parker?"

"Yes, good morning, sir. I'm sorry to bother you so early."

"I've been at the office since seven fielding calls. I'm sure you know what the subject matter is."

"Yes, sir. That's why I'm calling."

"I'd like to speak to you and the Board in person. I'm not a cheater. I want the chance to clear my name."

"That's very admirable, Parker. I'll be in touch."

Feeling like a man taking back control—I slip on a shirt and get to work. Hitting my smartwatch to track my workout, my bare feet pound across the sand. Maybe, just maybe—I'll be able to turn this shit around and have one last summer to be just me—Gabe, the guy who lives on the beach and works as a rent-a-cop. Because if things work out—a year from now, I'll be at a training camp getting my balls busted in pre-season for the pros.

FIVE

CALLIE

MY FIRST CUP OF COFFEE is a morning ritual. It's always black and strong enough to take the hair off a man's chest. I usually drink it outside watching the breaking waves when the weather's good.

"Morning, sweetheart."

"Hey Dad," I reply blowing on my coffee before taking a tiny sip.

"I need to talk to you." He takes a seat next to me on the stone sea wall.

"It's Mom, isn't it?"

His eyes cut away from the water to look at me. "It is. But it's not what you think."

"She's slowly doing better. But I can't keep running back and forth from here to the medical center at UVA. Especially since it's almost the height of the season. Traffic is going to be a bitch."

"It already is."

"I rented an apartment a few blocks from the hospital.

Charlie is going to spend time with Gran at her place in Delaware, and then I found a few cool camps for him by UVA."

"What about the café? And the marina?"

"That's where I need you. I know it's a lot, but you've been working at both since you were a kid. I couldn't leave the businesses in better hands."

My shoulders slump with all the weight he just put on them. "I-I'm supposed to take a few courses over the summer. I've already registered."

"I know. Gina's going to help with the books. The same crew from last year's back. We're fully staffed, and I trust you. I know you can do this."

Looking back out to the water, I take another sip. "You can count on me. Take care of Mom. We'll figure the rest out."

He puts a hand on my shoulder, turning to leave. "Stop by the marina first. I'll give you the passwords and go over the accounting software. The café is much less complicated to run."

"Okay."

With my legs dangling over the sea wall, I contemplate who I am. Daughter, sister, marina manager, café' worker, student, and after last night—a dirty slut.

I almost wish I had time for a summer fling. But too much is riding on me, and I won't let my family down. Picking up the house phone, I dial the hospital punching in my mother's room number.

"Hello?" her voice is soft, tired. I squish down any resentment I momentarily felt at all the responsibility that just was dumped on me.

"Hey, Mom. I wanted to call and say good morning. I know Dad and Charlie are coming up today, but I need to stay here—"

"And manage the businesses," she finishes for me.

"Yeah," I laugh.

"Oh, Callie. I've been thinking so much about you... I-I'm sorry. I wanted you to spend your summers at the beach, hanging out with your friends, not being forced to pick up our slack."

"Stop. Stop right there, Mom. Nothing matters but you— coming home."

"I hope that I do."

"You will."

"Well, when I do. I'm going to make this up to you. We'll get up early and stay up late. Binge on *The Crown* and popcorn and when we wake up, we'll walk the beach and find more shells for our collection. Then we'll go to Kiki's spa and get the works. After that, we'll have lunch on the boardwalk and gorge ourselves on crab cakes and lobster fritters."

"I've missed you." My hand puts the phone down, so she won't hear the sob that escapes. Swiping a tear, I take a deep breath, finding my cheery voice.

"Did you watch the royal wedding?"

"I sure did. I thought she looked beautiful."

"She did," I agree. "But the dress she wore to the second reception was even better."

"You'll find your prince too, sweetie."

"I don't need a prince, Mom. I'm doing just fine."

"Okay, who is he?"

"He's no one... shit! How do you do that? You always know!"

"Even though I'm not there... I know you better than anyone. It was in your voice."

"He's just some summer guy. I don't even know his name."

"Your father was just *'some summer guy'*... look at us now."

"Yes, but you and Dad are *the exception to the rule*."

"Maybe. But remember this, Callie. You never know what's

really going on in someone else's life. Look at what's happening to our family. Maybe you should give this boy a chance. Don't punish everyone for what that snobby asshole Elliott did."

"Yeah... his name was a sure give away he was an entitled jerk."

"Don't beat yourself up about it anymore."

"I won't. It's just... Sophie told me last night she saw him in town. His family came back for another summer."

"Just stay clear of him."

"I plan on doing exactly that."

"I love you."

"Love you, too, my sweet girl. Thank you for taking my mind off the damn pain."

"I'm coming to see you soon. Maybe even this weekend."

"You can't. It's Memorial Day. You're needed there."

"Well, then we'll video chat."

"Just warn me first so I can put my wig on."

"Stop, Mom."

"I'm serious. I don't want to scare you."

"The only thing that scares me is losing you."

"Ugh, the doctors are here. Doing their morning rounds. Go get that summer boy and have some fun."

"Okay. I'll think about it."

"Love you."

"Love you, forever," she answers hanging up.

Feeling better, I hop down and get ready to work. It's going to be a long, back-breaking summer, but maybe Mom's right. Letting my hair down with my sexy stranger just might be what I need.

"Cawwlie?"

"Morning Buddy. How did you sleep?"

"Good."

Charlie holds his favorite stuffed shark to his chest,

toddling down to me. He's five and a half but still so much a baby.

Mom panicked the closer she got to forty and the next thing I knew I was in high school swaddling my baby brother.

"Can you make some pancakes?"

"Absolutely." I ruffle his hair leading him inside.

Pouring him some fresh orange juice to drink while I mix the batter I turn to him. "Hey, bud. Dad tells me you, and he are moving to the city for a few weeks."

"Yeah," he drops his face in his hand, "I don't want to go."

"I know. I'm going to miss you a ton. But do you know who misses you more?"

"Mama."

"Yes. She misses you so much. I just talked to her, and she can't wait to see you."

"But I don't want to go to camp. I want to stay here and play on the beach."

"I know. What if... I come to get you one weekend and me, and you can hang out and boogie board all day?"

"Okay."

Feeling my chest tighten, I hold him close, bury my nose in his hair feeling like another piece of my heart's taking a bruising.

"Come on Callie. Come out tonight. You can't stay home depressed and lonely another night. It's opening night at Beachcomber. We're on the VIP list."

Feeling the oppressive weight of emptiness stuffing me down on the bed—my eyes flit towards the clock.

It's not even eight.

I'm snuggled in, wearing a ratty T older than dirt, while

feeling even older than that. Dad and Charlie left four days ago taking all the sounds of a home with them.

"Fine. But I'm not getting dressed up."

"Be ready in an hour. Nobody shows up before ten anyway."

Sighing, I fling my duvet off, shivering as the cold air hits my bare legs. I can't sleep without a thick blanket covering me like a cocoon, so the thermostat is always set to sixty.

I took a shower before I crawled into bed and my long hair hangs in waves from being air dried. Grabbing a pair of jean shorts, I slip them on, replacing my old T-Shirt with a simple tank. The only bits of flash are my favorite dangly earrings made from mother of pearl.

Spritzing my wrists with my favorite light perfume, I apply some gloss and mascara, place some bangles on my wrists, and grab my Coach wristlet.

Slipping on a comfortable pair of flat sandals, I grab my phone, keys, ID, and cash just as Soph knocks twice on my back door. I grin, feeling better already.

"Do you want to walk or drive?"

"Drive. My feet are killing me after waiting tables all day."

My eyes lower to her crazy heels. "Wearing those won't help."

She turns one leg out, "but don't they make me look damn sexy?"

"They sure do," I grin locking up.

We climb into my parent's summer car; an old convertible Dad fixed up years ago.

With the top down, my bestie by my side, and a night that feels as if something's in the air—my belly flips with excitement. The first night of summer always does this to me.

Even if I know better.

Even if I know magic isn't real.

Tonight, it feels like it is as cars line both sides of the small strip with the bass from a dozen different beats mixing. Horns honk as friends pass one another. I grin yelling, "Woo-hoo!" to a group of summer boys that pull up beside us in a beat-up Jeep Wrangler.

They holler back not noticing the light changed from red to green. My foot punches the gas, and we laugh, leaving them in the dust.

"See? I knew you'd have fun."

Sophie was right. I'm so glad I didn't miss opening night. I'm not putting myself on display like the dozens of single girls here, hanging in groups, with a drink in hand gyrating their hips, showing the men what they've got.

Standing under one of the twenty or so potted palm trees, driven up I-95 from Florida every year, turns the club into something that transports you to Miami... I feel the beat of summer running through me as my body moves to the rhythm the DJ's spinning.

"I'll be right back—going to get another round," Soph shouts over the music and the crowd.

Nodding, my eyes turn back to the crowded dance floor.

"Hello."

A finger taps my shoulder, causing me to turn, coming face-to-face, with *him*; my handsome stranger who kisses like a devil and looks like a naughty prince. He's wearing a ball cap low over his face, but his amber eyes beam like lasers as they zero in on me.

Behind him are two huge guys eyeing me like they are in on some secret—smirking like two idiots. I can't help but smile brightly.

"What? My friends get a bigger hello than me?" He whispers in my ear, index finger rubbing up and down my forearm gently before he takes my hand, leading me away.

"Soph?!" I call back over my shoulder. She waves me off, having found a group of old friends from high school we haven't seen in years.

My hand feels tiny in his as his big body parts the crowd. He leads me to the far corner of the dance floor by the stage, wraps his arms around me and slow dances to a song everyone else is cutting loose to.

He smells divine.

His aftershave and cologne are nice, but the smell of his laundered shirt makes me feel gooey and warm as he holds me close to his beating heart.

"This isn't so bad is it?" His hand is splayed against my tailbone holding me close pressing me against his muscular thighs. It's impossible not to feel him against me.

My nipples peak in my bra.

He's just so overpowering. Intense. Manly as fuck.

I don't answer, caught up in the spell of the first night of summer. He's a dark mage casting spells of lust and need on me.

His hands cup my face, mine cover his as he leans down, lips hovering, "who are you?" He looks pained as if not knowing who I am physically hurts. I don't answer. He lets out a breath, cupping my face hard, capturing my lips, kissing me like he's dying; thirsting for the taste of my mouth. We moan, hips pushing and pulling apart, grinding on the dance floor like a couple of drunks dry-fucking.

But if we're drunk—it's from the taste of each other's tongues and the crackling sparks shooting everywhere our bodies touch.

Taking his hand, I lead him past the bouncer, down a few

steps to the sand—feeling wild and reckless. I want his hands and mouth on me before I need to go home and be the responsible one.

I don't want more than this—don't have time for heartache. I'm not sure he's even looking for more than to put out the fire of passion blazing between us anyway.

With the waves breaking in the background, the moonlight spilling on us, the noise from the crowded bar behind us—he kisses me like I'm his lost love come home.

He's a rake, a handsome devil, with a body cut from steel, seducing me so skillfully—I wonder how many women have felt the magic of his touch.

He groans, hands cupping my ass, lifting me up. He walks me over to one of the massive pillars under the pier and backs me up against the rough wood.

His fingers trace my cheekbone, eyes beg, "who are you? Baby, please. I need to know whose face haunts my dreams every night."

Sighing, my hands stroke his sculpted jaw wishing I could just let him carry me off somewhere dark and mysterious and plunder my body like a pirate in a Regency Romance.

"Fuck it. Fine, don't answer." His breathing ragged as he runs a hand through his hair pissed and turned the fuck on as he stares at me.

"Don't. Don't be mad. My life...*it's complicated.*"

"So, uncomplicate it."

He reaches for me, taking both of my hands raising them above my head as his body pins me to the pole, mouth finding my neck.

"Yield to me, sweet princess. Tell me where to find you."

My head hangs, refusing to meet his eyes

I'll break if I do.

But I just don't have time for whatever this is burning

between us. Besides, I know when the days get shorter and colder everything will change. He'll move on, leaving me with nothing but memories full of nights like this. And I don't want to be that girl anymore—the one who gets left behind.

"I should go."

He steps back, the corded muscles of his neck flexing as he stares at me, trying to figure out what in the hell my problem is.

Brushing past him, I take a few steps before turning back. "It's not you. It's me."

His lips twitch. "Really Fanny? I've used that line a hundred times, and finally, someone's thrown it back. I should warn you—" He stalks closer, fists buried in the pockets of his khaki shorts. "... that I never lose. In fact, throwing down the gauntlet only makes me want the win more."

"You think seducing me is some game? That I'm some prize?"

Anger replaces passion as my eyes go dark.

"No Fanny. You're the missing piece of my heart."

"You're incredible. You are either a complete pyscho or the best player on campus. Maybe drunk girls believe the lies."

"Oh. It's not a lie sweetheart. I've been with enough women to recognize the real deal when I see it. And *you*—are the *REAL DEAL*. I don't need lines, Fanny. In fact, most days I need to pry talons off me. I'm kind of a big deal."

"Really?" My eyebrow arcs. "Well, good for you. I'm not interested in another player. So, if you think, I'm going to be impressed—don't forget I've already heard your lackluster singing and witnessed your lack of driving skills."

"I'm an excellent driver, especially when a woman's the wheel. My hands can be at six and twelve at the same time. Or if you prefer three and nine... I can do that too."

I try to hold it in.

I really do.

But he's so friggin cute, funny, and kisses like a Greek God. My lips part, with the grin, I tried to hide. "Oh yeah? What if I prefer going in reverse?"

His smile fades. "Don't tease me."

Striding forward, he takes me by the wrist, spins behind me pulling me tightly against him.

Taking a fistful of my hair, he sweeps it aside, lips finding the base of my neck. "I like reverse, too. It's one of my favorite ways to... *drive*."

Gasping at the image of him taking me from behind, I melt against him. My hands wrap over his as his lips find my ear. "Go. Go run. I'll give you a head start. If I find you in the same spot where I saw you earlier—you're coming home with me. No names, no questions—just the promise of a night filled with the sweetest, dirtiest, and roughest sex. I'll even make you pancakes in the morning."

"Gee, what an offer. I'll think about it. It's not every night an offer of a one-night-stand includes breakfast."

He smirks, "It's not every night the girl I want to take home refuses. But I assure you—once I have you in my bed—you'll never want to leave."

"Cocky much?"

"Always."

Shaking my head, I turn to go, "sex is overrated. It's never as good as you think it's going to be."

"Oh, sweetheart. It is. I promise—I don't know what douchebags made you think otherwise. But I know for sure— you and I are going to burn hotter than the volcano in Hawaii, and when we erupt—it's going to shoot us both beyond the stars and back."

"Damn you are good."

"The best, *sweet thang*."

"I don't know whether to laugh or swoon."

"How about both?"

I start running.

"One!"

He calls out.

"Two!"

I trip catching myself right before I face plant in the sand."

"Three!"

Looking like an ass, I bend down to slip my sandals off.

"FOUR!"

A screech leaves my mouth as I look back at him rocking like a sprinter on the race block.

"FIVE! I'm going to catch you sooner or later! Stop fighting it!"

Taking off, I sprint across the sand, flashing the bouncer the neon orange bracelet they gave me when I paid to get in, looking frantically for Sophie.

"SIX!" His roar stops some of the dancers as it rips through the night.

"Sophie!" I practically scream, stumbling past people, mumbling apologies as I grab her hand. "We've got to go. NOW!"

She takes one look at my panicked face and grabs her purse.

Racing to the parking lot, I vault right into the driver's seat of the convertible yelling at Soph to dive into the passenger seat.

Turning the key in the ignition, the powerful engine roars as I catch his hot eyes in the rearview as I peel out so hard—the tires squeal mixing with the tunes blaring from the car speakers, "The Boys of Summer by the Atari's."

He jogs after us, singing the lines, *"I can see you... your brown skin is shining in the sun..."*

"Please tell me you weren't running from him? Hit the brakes, Callie. What's wrong with you?"

"I don't know. He scares the shit out of me, though."

"Why?"

"Because he makes me feel wild, out of control. *Needy*."

"That's exactly why you should turn this car around."

Instead, my foot presses the gas harder.

I'm running.

Running as if the safety of my guarded heart depends on it. Because I know if he caught me—it'd be more than hot sex—he'd be the wave that would drag me under, refusing to let me free. I'd be caught in a riptide of desire, unable to break loose for the safety of shore.

I'd drown in him.

And I can't afford to do that again.

My first summer love took me years to rebound from.

I blame it on the dozens of Hallmark movies I've binged watched. The thing is—I am a believer in true love, rooting for the princess in the fairytale to live her happily ever after.

I'm just not sure I'll ever be her.

I'm more like Cinderella waiting on others all day but without the wicked step-mother. Without any family at all. Just an empty house where the ghosts of happier times linger.

GABE

"Who in the hell was that?"

"Fanny."

"Fanny? Are you shitting me?"

My eyes never leave the taillights in the distance. "Nope."

"Well, hell, what did you do to make her run like that?"

"I kissed her."

Marcus spews his beer all over the parking lot. Some of it

landing ten feet away on my flip-flops. "Damn. Dirty Player lost his mojo."

Trey and Marcus hoot hysterically at me standing by the road, taking the loss.

"Nah. She just couldn't handle the heat I was bringing."

"Well, she was hot. I mean like that chick Nina Dobrev from the Vampire Diaries." Marcus pauses realizing what he just confessed to, then shrugs. "What? They don't let you charge porn when we're on the road at away games. I needed something to spank it to."

Shaking my head, my eyes cut over to him when her car's out of view. "Don't you ever see her face in that perverted head of yours. She's going be my girl."

"Yeah, if you ever catch her."

"Shut up. Marcus. Come on, looks like you need another beer since you spewed yours all over the God damn place."

They clap me on the back as I adjust my hat low. We're getting plenty of stares, people on the verge of figuring out who we are. They know we are somebody by our huge builds and wide shoulders. The three of us together are deadly panty droppers. In fact—that's how the first few years of college went. But I've changed. These two buffoons might not have, but we're still tight and would do anything for each other.

"Check your phone."

Trey tells me as we shuffle back towards the bar. Opening it up, I read the new text message from him.

It's of us.

Me and Fanny, arms locked, bodies fused as we're lost staring into each other's eyes on the outdoor dance floor. He captured the moment, and now I have a picture of the girl whose taste is on my tongue, the scent of her still in my nose, and her beautiful face permanently etched in my head. I have a feeling her name will soon be tattooed on my heart.

SIX

CALLIE

MY FACE HEATS EVERY TIME I remember how I acted last night. In the moment—it felt wild and free just to let myself go. But now my cheeks burn with embarrassment. I can't believe I made out with him again.

I can't believe I ran.

"Rise and shine!"

"Gina?"

"I let myself in and brought breakfast."

She dangles a bag with the Krispy Kreme logo on it in front of my sleepy face. They are my weakness. I have a raging sweet tooth which is another reason why I bike instead of drive everywhere.

Following her down to the kitchen, I take a seat at the counter watching as she brews a pot of coffee.

"I'm worried about you. I understand why my brother took Charlie up to UVA, but it's not right to leave you here doing the job of two people."

"It's fine. I'm fine."

"Bullshit. How can you be?"

Shrugging, I look down, tracing invisible lines on the counter with my finger.

"Talk to me. I haven't seen you cry since Wes called you piggy tales in the fourth grade and yanked your braids out."

"I kicked him in the balls. I remember that was my first and last trip to the principal's office."

"I know this must be hard on you—"

"It is. But helping where I can, here... makes me feel like I'm doing something. At least I'm working—keeping the café and marina operating so we can afford to give Mom the best care."

"That doesn't leave you much time to date. Or go out with your friends."

"Dating's overrated."

She leans back, cocking her hip out to the side. "I'm only fifteen years older than you. Spill. What's going on Callie? You know you can talk to me."

Sighing, I meet her gaze. "Elliott. He—hurt me, badly."

"I know. Everyone usually gets badly burned by their first love. But you have to keep going—to find your real one."

"I know I was only eighteen. But the summer I spent with him was magic... at least at the time, I thought it was. It's been hard, staying here, seeing—remembering every place we went and all the things we did together. He just up and disappeared on me. Left like a wisp of smoke without a call or text. No goodbye. What a way to break up with me. I—he took my virginity."

"I figured."

"It hurt. Didn't feel good at all."

"I'm sorry. But when you have sex with a man that knows what he's doing—you'll never want to stop." She turns as the coffee machine beeps, pouring two fresh, hot steaming cups.

"I met someone new... but I'm scared to get hurt again."

"That's understandable. But you need to get yourself out there. Have you even dated anyone in the last two years?"

"Not really. I went out with a few guys here and there but nothing serious."

"Tell me about this new guy."

"He's built. I mean he's huge. I feel dainty standing next to him. He says the most ridiculously cheesy lines to me, but when he says them, I believe every word. And…. When he kisses me—I get lost in my own head. Like total brain freeze."

"What's his name?"

"I don't know. I keep running from him."

"Oh, Callie," she shakes her head, "that's only going to make him want you more. Men love a good chase."

"Oh? I was just scared of getting hurt. I'm not looking for a summer fling."

"Maybe one would be good for you."

"No. I can't handle that. My heart always gets in the way."

"You do have a big one. That's why everyone loves you. I need to open the bike shop. Don't be a stranger okay? I'm always here if you get lonely or need to talk."

"Thanks. I love you."

"Love you, too." She gives me a quick hug then places her empty mug in the sink. I walk her out, pondering her words. But I'm a chicken. My heart's already bruised and battered and wistful. Hoping my mother pulls through, it can't handle a man who came out of nowhere demanding things from me I'm not ready to give.

SEVEN

GABE

IT SHOULD'VE DIED DOWN, but it didn't. Instead, the press is even more obsessed with me than Jackie is.

Disappearing has only led to more rumors.

But no one in Sea Spray has discovered who I am... *so far.* Of course, using my last name as my first helps, especially if someone tries to look me up on the Internet.

"Parker, what's up?

"Hey Banger, how's it going?" I grin clasping his hand and taking a seat.

"Good. I got promoted at WBFN."

"That's great."

"And...," he leans in closer, "If you are wondering why I spend my days hiding out at the campus library it's because I'm the hottest DJ in town. Unfortunately for me though, the local girls know where I live."

"Yeah, I figured since everyone calls you, Banger. Did you grow up in Sea Spray?"

He shrugs, sipping his coffee, "So what? Every girl dreams of a summer fling. I just give them six weeks' worth in one night. And no, I'm from Georgia. I get free rent for spinning at the only real club in town."

"The Beachcomber?"

He nods.

"Well, I'm flying solo this summer. I'm focusing on getting myself back on track, so I won't be going out bar hopping."

"Smart plan... *Gabe*."

"Fuck, you know who I am?"

"Please. I might be into music, but I'm still a guy who grew up in the South and lived and breathed football for years."

"Shit."

"Hey, it's cool. I just thought I'd tell you in case you need a friend in town."

"Thanks. There is this girl I met the first night I came here."

"Yeah," he laughs, "there always is."

"No. But I like her. She was different, didn't have a fucking clue who I was and .... she ran from me. *Twice*. I don't know her story, but I want to write myself in it."

"Ouch. Maybe you have no game, as an *ordinary guy*."

"Bullshit. I have *game*. She wants me. There' s just something in the way. I need to find out what it is and crush it."

"What's this girl's name?"

I look down mumbling.

"What? I didn't catch what you said."

"I don't know," I mutter.

He cracks up. "This is priceless. Gabe Parker has a crush on a girl who runs away from him, and he doesn't even know who she is?"

"Yeah, that about sums it up."

He stares at me for a few seconds. "Ah, the age-old thrill of the chase and all that. I get it. Listen..., I have an idea..."

"Fuck, okay. I'm listening."

"Come on my morning show. Not as you... but as Parker Wells. The bullshit name you're going by. Talk to her. Live on the air. The town will eat this shit up and just maybe... she'll come to you."

"What if she doesn't hear?"

"She will," he sits back all confident and smug, "every shop in town listens to my show. Hell, it's streamed live at the lifeguard stations on the beach. If she doesn't hear it, someone that knows her will. If there's one thing I know about women—they talk to their girlfriends."

"Okay, what the hell. I'm in. But only if you keep helping me study for my exam retake."

"Of course, I will. It's so much bullshit what you're going through."

"Thanks. Who knew the resident DJ was such as badass at Calculus?"

"I'm double majoring, in case the music thing doesn't work out. I'll be able to fall back on my math degree. You're already good at it. I'll just help you be a bit better. You'll ace that test and be back on the field for senior year. Just don't forget me when you go pro."

"Hell, no. I'll send you VIP tickets for helping me. Hell, if you find my girl, I'll get you into the Super Bowl."

"Damn. She must be something."

"She... she could be everything."

"What? You only met her once."

"Twice. And sometimes that's all it takes. She went toe-to-toe with me, kissed like a sea siren and smelled like coffee and chocolate."

"Damn. Maybe I'll find her first."

"The fuck you will."

"What does she look like anyway?"

"Like a fucking angel. Mid-length dark hair that curls at the tips, light eyes that shoot daggers or fire depending on what's running through her head, toned legs and breasts...," I pause, fidgeting in my seat, getting hard just remembering how she felt and tasted beneath me.

"Okay... I get the picture," he laughs.

"Good, because I won't be able to concentrate with a woody."

"Fuck. Let's get to work then."

For the next three hours, Banger teaches me shortcuts. He has the mind of a genius. I'm looking at numbers and equations from a completely different angle. I'm more than ready to face the firing squad.

"You're ready."

"I think I am, too."

"Good. Go take care of this shit and then we'll find your girl."

"Thanks, man," I give him a fist bump, heading out to my car.

It's fucking sweltering out. If it weren't for the breeze coming off the bay, I'd think I was in the tropics.

My lips twitch imagining the look on Fanny's face when she hears me coming through the radio.

I hope her heart skips a beat like mine did when I realized it was her I had tackled down in the sand.

Taking out my phone, I scroll finding Coach's number.

"Parker?"

"Yeah. I'm ready."

"Good. I'll set it up and give you a date and time."

"Great. I'm digging Sea Spray. It's amazing."

"Yeah, I know. Are you taking good care of Gran's house?"

"Of course. I even water and weed the plants."

"She would've liked you son. You have integrity and a solid work ethic."

"Thanks. How long ago did she pass?"

"Ten years. But I didn't have it in me to change a damn thing in her house."

"Why would you? It's perfect. It feels like home. More of a home than I've had in years."

"Good. I expect your head and heart to be right for August. I need you to kick everyone's ass that got lazy over the summer in pre-season."

"You can count on that."

"Good," he grunts hanging up.

Walking through the small campus to the security building, I pause shaking my head and enter.

"Can I help you?" An older man built like a Mac Truck asks not even looking up from his desk.

"I'm here to pick up my uniform. I'm—"

"Gabe Parker. Holy fuck."

"Yeah, but this summer I'm just Parker. Parker Wells."

His mouth's still hanging open.

Great.

Sometimes the guy fans are worse than the girls. They want to talk plays, give me advice like they know the game better than I do.

"Well, hell. We're going to need to order you a special size. I don't have any uniforms that will fit. They never told me the star wide receiver was my new employee."

"Well, there was a reason for that."

"Shit son, the whole damn country is looking for your ass," he slaps his knee, "and here you are in my office."

"Yeah, imagine that."

"Sit. I have some paperwork for you to fill out. You want your pay direct deposited?"

"That'd be great. I'm still a broke college player."

"For now. I hear New England is looking at you. Heck—
you could end up on the Patriots bench."

"Hell no. I'll be on their field."

"First string, huh? You got balls."

"Of steel. I'm not busting my ass to be second best."

"Yeah. I see that. Can you start next week? The shift is six
to midnight."

"Sounds good to me."

Feeling cocky like all the stars are about to align, I leave his
office and head over to the small field house. It has a pool, a
weight room, and a part-time trainer.

It's all I need to complete the Gabe Parker summer plan to
conquer my world.

EIGHT

GABE

DRESSED IN THE LIGHT GREY SUMMER SUIT, I wore to my cousin's wedding last year—I'm ready to face them.

I asked to be given another exam: live. I'd take it in front of the board. They would score it then and there, seeing for themselves I didn't cheat. I know the information cold, and the professor wrote a new exam just for me. The president has it locked in his office, and I'm two hours away.

It's genius.

It came to me on my now nightly swim. It's become ritual and eases my sore muscles at the end of each day.

Truthfully, I look for her every night, hoping she'd show up again like a lucky star. Sea Spray is larger than it seems. The shops and restaurants on the main street are only a dozen at best, but the miles of sandy beach, inlets, coves, and hiking trails make this kind of a paradise.

I can feel the muscles in my legs have already gotten stronger from training on the beach and then hiking up every bluff. I feel like Rocky Balboa in his first movie—fighting some unseen foe, throwing jabs and right hooks, and training for the fight of his life.

In a way—I am. If I get expelled—there goes the NFL, my degree, and everything I've worked for years to achieve would instantly vanish. My mornings are full of conditioning, the afternoons spent in class, and at night I get to put on my rent a cop uniform going out on patrol.

It's better than I thought it would be. Who knew I'd be good at it? I've already become the rookie to hand out the most parking tickets and even saved a sea turtle who got lost.

I'm goddamn Rocky and Clark Kent. I've got mad super-powers, and nothing can stop me now.

Synching my phone to the car's radio, I get my jam on.

"Here I go again on my own...." Belting out Whitesnake like it's my track, I don't give a shit as I stop traffic in my designer suit, older car, and sick voice.

Fanny knows I'm good.

I just need to find her.

In fact, that's the next thing on my to-do list after I straighten out everything at UVA.

Hell, maybe I should give a music career a shot if football doesn't pan out.

"They're ready for you."

"Thank you." My long legs uncross, my hand instinctively straightening my navy-blue silk tie as I follow the secretary down the hall to a large conference room.

Twelve heads swivel in my direction. My feet slow and I look each person in the eye. "I want to personally thank every one of you for this opportunity to prove myself. I value this University very much. I would never want to tarnish its good name. On these grounds games were won and lost but this is not a game. My name is at stake and the future I've worked so hard for. Thank you for giving me a chance to save it."

Coach catches my eye and nods his head.

I sit at the only empty seat, and the chancellor unlocks his briefcase sliding the exam across the polished wood table.

The President sets a timer.

It's game on.

My forehead creased in concentration as my pencil makes notations and my fingers tap the calculator.

It's hard.

They made this exam yards harder than the previous two. But that's fine. My head is clear and my heart light.

It's easy to have a clear conscience when you're innocent. Lips twitching at the next equation, I make a mental note to buy Banger a few rounds. This was a set-up. Someone in this room wanted me to fail, and I would have if not for the luck of meeting one of the smartest math majors on campus.

Standing up, I shrug out of my suit jacket, unbutton my pressed shirt and roll up my sleeves. A small gasp has my eyes snapping to the corner where the Chancellor's student PA sits fidgeting with her skirt.

I wink.

"Dirty Player," she mouths biting her lip.

Sitting back down with a grin, I ace this shit, in a rush to get back to Sea Spray and find Fanny. I want to kiss her under the stars, wrap her in my blanket and wakeup cuddled next to her while the surf pounds nearby.

I finish with five minutes to spare even after I double checked my work. Silently, my hands slide the exam back to the other side of the table.

It's so quiet you could hear a pin drop. Professor Higley and President Yates both grade it in a murmur of low whispers. Finally, shaking her head in disbelief, her eyes meet mine.

"Congratulations Parker. You scored a 96."

"What? Where did I go wrong?"

Eagerly I ask for the paper back. Professor Higley cracks a wry smile, refusing to hand it over. "Sorry. This exam must remain a part of our larger investigation. I can tell you after this —you are in the clear for now. But we might call you to testify in front of the committee as part of the overall investigation into our student-athletes," President Yates informs me.

"Thank you, Sir. I understand."

Higley's lips thin as she reluctantly hands my exam to him to be locked back up.

Bingo.

She had it out for me.

I knew it.

Rising, I collect my things, place my suit coat over one arm, rounding the table to shake each hand one at a time; like a tycoon in a boardroom who just struck a major deal.

"Good job, son."

"Thanks, Coach," I reply as he slaps my back.

Feeling like a vindicated man, my feet practically skip back to my SUV.

"Gabe."

Fuck.

"Jackie."

Spinning around I face my ex.

"Where have you been?"

Arms crossed over my chest—I don't answer.

"I miss you."

"Yeah? Well, I don't miss you, sweetheart. I told you weeks ago we were done. How did you know I'd be here?"

"My sorority sister is the Chancellor's PA."

"Of course, she is," I reply remembering how she glanced at me.

"I need to leave. I have a job to get to."

"Please... give me five minutes. Can we talk?"

My jaw tics. "We don't work well, sweetheart. I don't party like you. I'm on track to be someone—someone big."

"I know."

"So that's what this is about? You wanted to attach yourself to a guy about to go pro and ride the wave with him?"

She averts her gaze, shifting her weight on her strappy sandals. "No. of course not. It's just...I've tried to get over you. But I can't. No one else can compare to you—in or out of bed."

"I haven't been with anyone since we broke up. Clearly you have. But I'd be done regardless. I'm sorry. I need to go."

Her face falls, realizing she said too much.

"Shit." A dozen reports race towards us obviously tipped off.

"GABE! Are you a part of the official investigation?"

"Do you regret not entering the draft last spring?"

"Gabe! Over Here! Will you be playing next season?"

Without a backward glance, I open my door, fire up the engine and roll down my windows grinning as Timberlake comes on. I sing "Cry me a River," along with him.

She flips me the bird; her face a fiery sunburn as I peel out leaving both her and the stunned reporters behind.

Maybe that wasn't the best idea. Most of why I dumped her is because of her psychotic mood swings. I'm hoping six more weeks apart might be enough time and space for her to move on. But somehow, I don't think moving to the other side of the world would be far enough for her to be able to let this go.

My phone rings through the Bluetooth just as I hit the highway.

"Banger! What's up? I crushed it. I nailed the test, man. I owe you a beer."

"Congrats. That's friggin awesome. But I was calling to see if you're free on Wednesday morning? I want to put you in the line-up, and we can do a shout out to your mystery girl."

My heart thumps in my chest. Christ, why in the hell did I waste time with Jackie? No girl has made my heart pound, or my palms sweat like this.

"Do it. Text me the address to the station and I'll be there."

"Good. I come on at nine so show up at eight."

"Great, see you then."

Two days.

In two more days, she'll hear me. I hope she answers.

NINE

JACKIE

I'VE NEVER FELT SO HUMILIATED as I did when Gabe left me standing on the hot pavement with news trucks and camera crews catching him diss me on tape. When it was clear they couldn't catch up with him—they turned to me.

I'm about to give them the story they are looking for. I hide my smug eyes under my new Tory Burch sunglasses. Gabe was so busy singing like an idiot—something that always got on my nerves that he never noticed the car at the far corner of the lot that pulling out behind him after I gave a head nod.

I'll find him. Tip-off TMZ and cash in. But first, I'm going to tell the press... *our story.*

At least the way I saw it.

If I can't have him—no one will want him after I drag his name through the dirt. I came to UVA looking for a ring. I'm not going to work at some dead-end desk job. When I met Gabe, I knew I found my trophy husband. He's a champ—on and off the field, a voracious lover with the body of an Olympic athlete, and he's smart.

Too smart.

I knew I was losing him and tried everything to keep him, but it only made him let go more.

Maybe if my plan works, I could be the next bachelorette. In fact, I'm banking on it. With my best quivering lip and crestfallen face, I turn to the cameras.

"I'm Jackie. Jackie Delaware, Gabe's ex-girlfriend. I've been trying to get him to stop, begged him for months to stop doping. But he wouldn't listen. His grades started slipping... and he did it. Cheated on everything. I tried to help him, but he pushed me away..."

TEN

CALLIE

THE PAST FEW WEEKS FLEW by in a blur. I helped pack up Dad and Charlie then started working fifteen-hour days. By the time I crawled into bed each night completely drained, it was time to get back up again.

Tonight's my first class: Organic Chemistry.

I'm doomed. But I don't have a choice and no one to complain too. My mom didn't ask for cancer, and we're barely paying off the insurance co-pays.

I can't let my family down.

It's the height of the season. The money that we make now carries us for the rest of the year.

Clipping on my fanny pack that contains my wallet, keys, and cell, I peddle from my morning shift at the café over to the marina until it's time for class. With the amount of traffic buzzing by, it'll be faster than driving and keeps my legs toned.

The marina's been in the family for three generations. When it's not busy, I can at least study in the back office.

"Hey Callie, looking good."

"Hey, Wes. What's up?" Smiling at him, I hop off my bike, walking down the dock.

"Well... I'd be embarrassed to tell you what. If you keep coming by wearing those tight white shorts."

"Stop. You're my employee."

"So? You are the hottest chick in town."

"Stop flirting and get back to work. Before I have to fire you."

"Shit. That'd be hot. Would you be all strict and bossy? Cause I could go for that." He swaggers towards me, hose in hand.

"Don't you dare!"

He winks pressing down on the nozzle. "Wes!" I shriek stumbling back as a spray of cold water hits my chest. "You're going to pay for that."

His eyes go wide, looking behind me, but I'm not falling for that trick.

Instead, I fall back into a strong pair of tanned arms that wrap around my wet waist. They tighten, and I'm struck at how tan the man's hands are against my white shirt. But then the smell of Polo cologne kicks me in the gut.

Elliot.

Jerking out of his hold, I hide my shaking hands by twisting the ends of my shirt with them.

"Callie," he breathes looking at me like I'm not a ghost, but an angel.

"Elliot? This is a surprise. Does my small town bore you already? Decided to go out slumming? Well, I'm not interested."

"Actually, I wanted to rent a fishing boat."

Face flaming, my hand gestures over to Wes. "Fine. He can help you with that."

Spinning on the heel of my converse sneakers, I walk down the rest of the dock with as much dignity one can manage after a surprise run-in with a former flame while wearing a soaked shirt while smelling like fried hash browns and coffee.

Grabbing the clipboard hanging off a nail tacked on the last post on the pier, my eyes scan the tide charts, and latest Coast Guard report. My back is towards him, but I feel his eyes on me.

Refusing to turn around, I hang the clipboard back up and enter the small office where we also sell bait and tackle.

My father's cap hangs on the wall. Sitting in his old squeaky chair gives me comfort. The familiar smell in here helps me feel secure: diesel fumes and dead fish.

Yeah, Elliot Langston and I have nothing in common. Our worlds would have never mixed, but hormones didn't understand that. Neither did my teenage heart.

Sighing, the corner of my eyes flit to the windows. Wes upsold him. Led him straight over to the most expensive boat we have for rent. My father paid three hundred thousand for it. My Mom didn't speak to him for weeks and me—*I had the time of my life taking it out to sea.*

She moves fast, can handle any wave short of a hurricane, and is sexy as fuck.

Sheena.

That's the name painted in scripted neon purple on the stern. I snort, remembering that's another thing that pissed Mom off. He named the boat after an eighties pop star who wore stretch leotards and headbands and not his wife.

My eyes flit from the boat to Elliot.

He's more built than he was two years ago...taller, too. He's hot. Hot like a man with money is; all polished boat loafers, khaki shorts, and crisp polo shirt. He carries himself regally like he was born into something greater than the rest of us.

I didn't know what it was then. But I see it clearly now: he's American royalty, born into one of the oldest families in the South. It screams from every pore in his body.

They both suddenly turn to look at the office, Wes gestures for Elliott to wait.

"What happened?" Wes walks in somberly, clearly something was said, "was I too harsh?"

"It's not that—although you were a bit of a bitch."

"Yeah, I was."

"He wants it. For the whole season."

I whistle. "Doesn't his family already own a yacht?"

"We do. But my brother's sailing it up to Maine."

My eyes snap to the door where Elliot silently stands.

"Fine. Let me crunch some numbers. In the meantime, feel free to take it out for the day. I'll need a credit card and ID in case you sink the damn thing."

"I have a Captain's license. From the Naval Academy in Annapolis."

"Of course, *you* do," I smile sweetly taking his card and licenses, photocopying them.

His honey brown eyes are puzzled as he stares down at me utterly clueless as to why I can't stand him. He could've at least tried to make my first time better.

"You're all set. Here's the keys. Keep the Coast Guard channel on the radio and call us if you have any issues. We close at six. She's due back in port by five."

"Yes, Ma'am," he smirks.

Our fingers brush as he takes the keys.

But I don't feel sparks, see stars, or feel one tingle.

Thank God.

I keep busy for the rest of the day, helping Wes hose down boats that reek of dead fish and beer as they come back into the dock. The hardest part is doing it all with a smile. Taking a break, my fingers dig into the bottom of my fanny pack for loose change, and I plunk them into the beverage dispenser.

"Why don't you just get the key and help yourself? You own the machine."

I shrug. "I'm too thirsty and tired to take another step. You want one?"

"I'll take a Red Bull."

My finger presses the selection; two Red Bulls drop out the bottom.

"I have class later. I'll need the boost of caffeine." Popping the top, I tip my bottle to his. "To making our season already."

"What?"

"I crunched some numbers... if I charge seventy-five-grand for him to rent it out, I can pay off a solid portion of the loan and use the extra cash to help my Dad pay the medical bills."

He sips his Red Bull almost choking on it. "You think Elliot will pay that?"

"Well... I'm willing to waive the slip fee and give him a discount on the diesel."

"Maybe if you give him another chance... he'll pay more."

"I'm not whoring myself out, Wes."

"Noted. But he did ask if you were seeing anyone."

My eyebrow rises, "What did you say?"

"I said that I didn't know, but that you shot me down quickly."

"Well, that's because you dated Sophie."

"In junior high school. That hardly counts."

"It does. I won't break girl code."

"Fine. I'm hitting up The Beachcomber later anyway. The summer girls are all looking good so far."

The sound of a powerful engine humming through the water has me looking past him. Elliott stands behind the wheel up on the bridge. The breeze ruffles his hair, and before he catches me staring, I mumble something walking inside where I can hide behind paperwork.

Five minutes later the door swings open. I feel his eyes on me.

Continuing to ignore him, I pull up the forecast on my iPad.

"Can we talk?"

"Sure, I've printed the lease paperwork for Sheena. Does seventy-five thousand sound reasonable for four months? September is still warm, and we won't dry dock her until October."

"I didn't want to talk about the boat."

"Oh? I can't imagine there's anything else to discuss?"

He comes in softly shutting the door. "I thought about you for months."

"Really? I find that hard to believe when you left without even telling me you were going."

"I had no choice. My grandfather had a heart attack. He didn't make it, and the rest of the summer was over after that."

"Oh, I'm sorry to hear that. But you still could've called, texted—hell sent me a postcard."

"I know. A million apologies wouldn't suffice. But I did have feelings for you, Callie."

Nodding my head, eyes lowered, my hand pushes the paperwork forward.

He ignores it.

"Let me take you to dinner."

"I can't."

"Can't or won't?"

"Both."

"Fine. I'll be back." He snaps the paperwork off the desk,

skims the pages, signs his signature with a flourish dropping a check in front of me for the full amount. He stares at me hard with his jaw ticking, as if he wants to say more but instead he shakes his head and leaves.

The breath I didn't even know I was holding exits in a whoosh. My hands shake as I pick up his check. He added twenty-five thousand to what I had asked for.

Bewildered, heart pounding, I feel sick. Does he know? About my family...about Mom?

I can't cash this.

It feels wrong.

Not sure what to do, I unlock the small safe bolted to the floor placing the check inside.

"Callie? I'm punching out. My shift's over."

"Shit!" Grabbing my pack, my eyes flit to the clock on the wall.

I have five minutes to get to campus before my class starts at six.

"I'm never going to make it. I biked here."

Wes forks over the keys to his prized refurbished Mustang. "I insist. Take it."

"Thanks! I owe you a million," my lips land on his cheek as I fly out the door sprinting down the dock.

———

My head was spinning for the first half hour, but I finally settled in and started taking notes with the borrowed pencil and paper I got from a friendly face in the class.

The sky outside bloomed with the pink and oranges hues of the sunset before turning to twilight where the stars came out to shine. Now, the horizon's inky black with the clouds hiding half the moon.

With the keys to Wes' car tightly in my hand, the soles of my shoes clack on the pavement. I stop looking both ways before crossing the road into the parking lot.

Shit.

The campus police busted me.

"No! Wait I can explain!" I shout running towards Wes' car as the tow truck driver attaches chains to the undercarriage.

The campus cop stands with his arms crossed not even glancing at me as I stop behind him.

He's huge. I haven't seen a guy this cut, tan, and filled out in my life.

"Excuse me? That' s my car."

"Then you are out of luck. You parked in one of the three handicapped spaces in the lot."

"I-I can explain, please."

He finally turns to face me.

"You!"

"Fanny?!"

We both shout at the same time.

He smirks, "The only way I'm letting you get out of this is if you tell me your name and give me a date."

"I don't date rent-a-cops. They're fake."

"Wanna see my badge?" He leans down, whispering against my hair.

"There's been a mistake. Please stop," I beg the tow driver as he finishes and moves toward the cab.

"Your name. I'm waiting."

Jerking my head towards my hot nemesis, I dig in. I don't know why. There's just something about him that ticks me off and turns me on at the same time. It twists my emotions into a knot and fucks with my head.

"What's yours?"

"Can't you read the name tag?" His finger points to the

cheap plastic tag pinned on his shirt that says, Parker. But I won't give him the satisfaction of letting him hear me say it.

"Say it."

"No."

"Fine." His hand helicopters in the air signaling for the driver to go.

"Asshole," I breathe, watching helplessly as Wes's car gets towed.

He's going to kill me

"So. It looks like your stuck with me. I'll give you a ride home for a kiss."

In ten seconds, I plot my next move.

Sauntering towards him, I stop just as the tips of my shoes, touch his. He inhales sharply, eyes blazing as he studies my face.

He wants me.

Bad.

My tongue comes out to lick my lips. "You're killing me," he groans, hands reaching for my waist.

Grabbing the back of his head, I tug it down to mine. "You weren't that good last time." I lie through my teeth, moving back and racing to the driver's side of the campus police car. He watches in stunned shock as I climb in, turn on the lights, lock the door, and pull away.

In the rearview, I catch him laughing so hard he cries. I roll down my window as I loop around out to the main road, sticking out my tongue at him.

He roars, "I think I just fell in love!" I flip him the bird. "Please! Your name!" He calls out jogging after me.

Laughing, I drive off. I don't know what it is about him. I forget the weight of all my responsibilities, how sick my mom is, and how lonely I am when I go home.

He turns me inside out and makes me feel alive.

Driving straight to the police station I park, walk straight inside past the security camera pressing the intercom button.

"Miss? How can I help you?" The cop on duty asks behind the bulletproof glass.

"I'm Callie. The Chief's niece. I need to turn myself in for stealing a car."

She laughs, thinking I'm joking. I walk through the maze of cubicles to the back hall where his office is. He's single and practically lives at the station. I knew he'd be here.

"Callie?"

"Hey, Uncle Steve. I committed a felony."

"Sure, you did," he snorts.

But his smile falls as I take a seat, with a deadpan face.

"Callie?"

"I stole a campus police car. But don't worry it's parked out front."

"Christ. Are you fucking with me?"

"No."

"Jesus? Whatever for?"

"He wanted a kiss."

"Who?"

"Some rent-a-cop, Parker. I borrowed Wes's car, and this cop guy was having it towed. But he said he'd let it go if I kissed him.

"So, you made option B."

"I did."

"He must've been some loser."

"Totally. A huge loser," I nod my head.

"Fine. I'll take care of it."

"Thanks."

"Just stay out of trouble for the rest of the summer, okay?

Jesus, you jacked a cop car?" He laughs at the thought. Once he starts, he doesn't stop.

We both laugh until we cry. It feels cathartic, like a cleansing. I've been keeping so much in, all my feelings about mom, Elliot, missing Charlie, that I'm finally able to release.

"Ah, shit." He wipes his face with a Kleenex and picks up his desk phone holding one finger up for me to keep it together.

"Benson? It's Chief Anderson. I hear you boys are down a cruiser... yeah, I have it. No, it wasn't stolen. We were just pranking your new rent-a-cop. I'll have someone drop it off."

"Uncle Steve?"

"Yeah?"

"I need one more favor...Wes' car, is still impounded."

"I'll have it released and driven to his house. Come on. I'll drop you home."

"Thanks."

He opens his drawer, picking up his keys, "she stole a cruiser? God, I wish I could've seen that" he talks to himself under his breath, motioning me to follow him out the back to the door.

We make chit-chat as he drives through town. Couples are out strolling hand in hand. Both our windows are rolled down, and the beat of the live band playing at The Beachcomber spills out into the night.

Sea Spray's alive with a vibe that only comes once a year. The air smells like waffle cones and food cooking on grills.

Closing my eyes, I make a promise to myself not to miss out on this anymore. The next time I see Parker, I'm going to plant a big wet one on him before someone else does. At least I know where to find him now.

We pull up at the curb to the home that's been in our family for decades, and I climb out.

"Don't be a stranger, Callie girl."

"I won't. Thanks!" I shut my door, waving as he drives off.

After a long hot shower, I pull on Parker's shirt, climb into bed, and lay awake listening to the sounds of summer. I let my mind float with the music and the breeze as I fall asleep remembering how Parker stared down at me like I was a gift just for him.

ELEVEN

GABE

I WOKE UP AN HOUR EARLIER than usual to get my work out in before meeting Banger at the radio station. Running in the sand gives so much more resistance than on a track. It's done wonders for the muscles in my legs. Sprinting the last quarter mile as fast as I can, I finish by diving straight into the ocean, under a breaking wave.

Nothing is up but me and the rising sun. The water cools my heated skin. I float for a bit before getting out and doing a series of planks and pushups.

Today is the first day of (OFH) Operation Find Her. And just like everything else: I won't accept anything less than a win. After my morning routine, I get right to the station

"You ready for this?"

"I've been waiting all week."

"Are you nervous?"

"Did you forget who I really am? I'm on the field in front of thousands of people. I have nerves of steel."

"Then why are you sweating?"

"It's hot as hell in this glass box."

"Gabe, the studio is ice-cold."

"Whatever. What do I do?"

He places headphones over my ear and points the green light above the door. "I'm going to introduce you at the beginning of the segment. When the green light turns on... we're live. I'll point to you when you're up."

"Sounds easy."

Banger puts on his on headphones and sits at the other mic. "Goood morning Sea Spray. It's Banger coming to you live on this happy hump day. I have a special guest live in studio with me suffering from a serious summer crush. I mean, I've never seen a guy so hung up on a girl he's just met. So, let's help him out Sea Spray. In the name of summer love, let's help my friend Parker find his mystery girl."

He points to me, and I speak straight from my heart.

"I want to tell you about this girl. I don't know her name, but I can't stop thinking about her. First she stole my breath, then she stole my clothes, my car and finally...my heart. Fanny, if you're out there...please put me out of my misery and go on a date with me. I'll be waiting for you every night where we first kissed. Parker."

The light turns red, Banger goes to commercial, and phones start ringing off the hook.

TWELVE

CALLIE

I'VE BEEN UP SINCE FIVE, brewing coffee and getting everything ready to open the café at six. It's almost nine but the middle of the week is mostly quiet until lunchtime.

Sophie wipes down tables as I clear some dishes. It's a beautiful morning, the waves are up, and I opened the back doors, letting the ocean wind blow through.

Reggae music plays on our local station. Sophie and I dance our way through the shifts on most days, listening to our resident bad boy Banger. No one knows his real name, or even where he came from. But he shows up every summer tearing through every girl in town, well, besides Soph and me. Neither of us joins "the scene." Both of us prefer watching from under the shadows of the palm trees at Comber's as we sip our drinks and watch the craziness.

"Gooood morning Sea Spray. It's Banger coming to you live on this happy hump day. I have a special guest live in studio with me suffering from a serious summer crush. I mean, I've never seen a guy so hung up on a girl he's just met. So, let's help him out Sea Spray. In the name of summer love, let's help my friend Parker find his mystery girl."

Soph and I both pause listening to Banger. She finds the remote turning up the volume to the wireless speakers.

"I want to tell you about this girl. I don't know her name. I can't stop thinking about her. First she stole my breath, then she stole my clothes, my car and finally...my heart. Fanny, if you're out there... please put me out of my misery and go on a date with me. I'll be waiting for you every night where we first kissed. Parker."

My feet stick to the floor as his rich, smooth voice comes on the air. My lips part, my hands clutching the rag I picked up in shock.

"Holy shit. It's you. He was talking about you!"

My heart beats as fast as a bird's wings. I feel hot and cold, nervous and flustered as hell.

"That was the most romantic thing I've ever heard." A woman remarks sipping her coffee.

"Callie!" Sophie hisses, grabbing my arm. "Call! Call Banger at the radio station right now. Get him, girl."

I shake my head, drop the dishrag I was clutching walking straight out the back door to the beach.

For the first time, I'm too stunned to make a move. He's outplayed me. I need to stop playing this game and admit I fell just as hard for him. I'll meet him but maybe not tonight. I'll make him sweat for one more day.

THIRTEEN

SOPHIE

MY EYES FOLLOW CALLIE walk like a zombie out the back door. Quickly surveying the small number of customers in the café, I reach inside my pocket for my phone.

Hiding behind the counter, where I can peek around the corner, keeping one eye on Callie—I make a call.

"WBFN, you're live with Banger."

"I know who she is," I blurt out.

"Sure, you do," Parker chimes in, "you're the hundredth caller claiming to either know or be my girl."

My eyes flit over to Callie's fanny pack on the shelf beneath the cash register.

"Her fanny pack. It's powder blue with sparkly polka dots. And I know that you still have her bike."

The line goes silent; then Banger comes on. "Don't hang up. I'm putting you on hold to cut to commercial."

"Well hurry up, she'll be back any second, and I'll be busted."

"She's there with you? Right now?" Parker asks sounding as if he's about to go apeshit.

The sound of Reggae music fills my ear. *Shit.* I'm on hold.

"Are you still there?" Banger asks coming back.

"Yes, But I need to be quick. I won't tell you her name, that's up to her. But I can tell you where to find her... but Parker, you better not screw this up or try any shit with her on the beach again until after a few proper dates."

"Yes, ma'am. Wait? She told you about that night?"

"Of course, she did. I'm her best friend."

"Admit it. She told you I kissed like a God."

"Maybe."

"So, if you won't tell me her name, can I know yours?"

"Sophie. Look I can't hang on, she works mornings at the Blue Hydrangea café on Main Street."

"Thanks, Sophie. I'll toast you at our wedding."

"You do that," I snort hanging up.

Callie's going to kill me. But it'll be worth it. She deserves a summer love more than anyone girl who ever lived.

Slipping my phone back in my shorts, I hum my way till noon.

"Why are you so chipper all of a sudden?"

"No reason. I just feel like something's on the edge of the horizon."

"Did you drink a triple shot of espresso, again?"

"No," I laugh. "Can't a girl just be happy?"

Callie shakes her head at me, untying her apron. "I'm off to the marina. Are you good here?"

"Yep. I know the drill. What are you going to do about Parker?"

"I'm thinking about it."

"Don't think too hard, he might tire of the chase."

She smiles, straps on up her pack and walks outside to the bike rack. I know I did the right thing, even if she makes me work doubles until September.

FOURTEEN

GABE

SHE DIDN'T SHOW LAST NIGHT, but I'm not worried. With the information Sophie gave, I used my mad hacking skills and looked up everything about the Blue Hydrangea. And there on the website was the story of the café and the owners...the Anderson's—including a picture of their daughter, *Callie*.

With that, I searched town records and found her address. She's not going to see me coming; it's just past dawn. Dew and the wetness from the ocean air cling to anything still out until the sun fully rises and takes it away. My eyes look to the sky where twinkling stars try to stay, but the growing light makes them slowly fade. Sitting in the sand, I work out the kinks from sleep stretching my muscles.

I wish I could stay here forever. No one bothers me. I can let my walls down without worrying about who's coming at me next, wanting either a piece of my impending fame and status or trying to rip it from my hands.

One thing I know for sure is she's a part of it. A big piece of how I'm feeling. She's funny as hell, brave, sweet, and so fucking beautiful. But she keeps slipping through my hands like sand. I've no doubt I'll catch her now that I know where to find her.

I've got the most completed catches in the end zone in college football, but somehow catching Callie is frustratingly hard.

But once I'm in the zone with my eye on the prize, nothing can stop me from making the play.

Scoring is what I do.

But I don't just want to score with Callie; I want to keep her. Make her my girl, and I can't wait to go back to campus knowing she's going to be there with me. But first, I've got to rewind the game tapes and start fresh with a date. It's going to be damn hard to pretend I haven't touched her, seen her perfect breasts and felt her nipples harden on my tongue.

Pounding the sand as I get up, I force that shit to the back of my mind.

With my game face on, my feet fly across the wet sand. I'm doing intervals today. After five minutes I stop getting down to pump out a hundred pushups getting the blood flowing to my biceps. I'm working out shirtless, so when I surprise Callie, she'll get a good look at what she could have—if she stops running. The circuit drill I'm doing with Turkish getups and planks will make my arms pop and hopefully, her body *melt*.

With a wicked glint in my eyes, I sprint down the sand towards 12 Sandpiper Lane.

My feet fly over the three miles of beach. Heart hammering, I slow to a jog, cut up the beach, and loop around to her block dropping on the sidewalk for fifty more pushups before peering through her front door.

It's not a small home, but like many here it's built up rather than out, making it easy for me to spot her through the open floor plan. She's sitting on a terrace wall facing the ocean.

Grinning, I pluck a rose from her neighbor's yard my feet silently walking through the cut grass.

"Good morning."

She sets down her mug, turning wide-eyed at me standing on her back patio holding out a rose.

She hesitates for a second.

My eyes flare as she stands, wearing my shirt and... nothing else.

Clenching my jaw, I slowly back up, counting out loud, "you slept in my shirt?"

She nods, looking down at herself. My T-shirt is large on her of course, landing just above her knees. But it's sexy as fuck that she's in it.

"You have six seconds to go inside and get changed before I kiss the breath out of you."

She doesn't move.

We stare each other down, eyes locked, hearts racing as I begin.

"*One.*"

Her lips fall open.

"*Two.*"

My fists clench.

"*Three.*"

The pulse at her throat hammers.

"*Four.*"

My dick jerks in my shorts.

"*Five.*"

She drops the rose.

"*Six.*"

We move at the same time, rushing into each other's arms.

Mouths are opening wide, our tongues fuse together, arms holding each other tight.

Holy fuck. I have butterflies.

This girl—gave me *butterflies.*

Her hands, grasp my head, holding me close as if I'm ever going to leave now that I've found her.

My hands lift her up. Spinning around, I brace her against the back of the house moaning into our kiss as her tan legs wrap around my waist.

My eyes roll back in my head as my dick hits the sweet spot between her thighs.

Even through my mesh shorts, I feel her heat and want more.

She moans, coming up for air.

"I knew I'd find you, Callie."

Her eyes smile at mine as she pulls me back and we kiss like long lost loves, the funny thing is: I feel like I just found mine. But she's not lost anymore; she's definitely found.

We kiss as if our souls are bound but have been separated for a thousand lifetimes.

Maybe they were.

"Callie...," I reluctantly pull back, backing away, "I need to go before I carry you inside and do things to you... that would make a hooker blush."

Her eyes drop, cheeks turning pink. She's sweet so sweet, making me want to drop to my knees and taste the rose between her thighs.

My fists clench as I force myself to back up. The impulse to carrying her down the beach and take her in the soft sand is becoming too hard to fight.

She bites her lip, brow furrowing, and I almost lose all self-control. She rushes towards me grabbing my hand. "You're bleeding."

"Am I?" Looking down, I notice the bright red prick I must've got from when I plucked the flower for her.

She takes my index finger in her tiny hands bringing them to her lips.

"Fuck, Callie," I hiss as she places it in her hot mouth sucking my injury as if her kiss could heal it. Watching her clean my wound with her tongue has got me so hard, my brain short circuits since all the blood went to my dick.

Picking her up fireman style, she screeches as I jog down the beach dumping us both into the surf.

She laughs splashing me, but my eyes are locked on her chest where my T-shirt clings to her like a second skin.

She comes to me, cups my face and says, "I'm not running anymore."

"Good. But I wouldn't stop chasing you anyway."

A wave crashes over us—my arms snag her waist pulling her in tight. "What am I going to do with you?"

"Kiss me."

Growling, my hands lift her hips, her legs wrap around my waist, feet braced apart, she groans into my mouth feeling how much I want her.

"I want you so bad, baby. But we're going to take this slow, even if it kills me." Taking her lips, my mouth crashes over her like a wave. She clutches my head kissing me back matching my tongue thrust for thrust. Her hips rock into mine. Making me want to break the promise I just made.

"God baby, you feel so good. Taste so sweet. You're doing wild things to me."

She pulls back, locking her feet tighter around my back. "You better not be feeding me lines. I've heard this kind of talk before."

My jaw clenches at the thought of another man's hands on her. "I'm the real deal, sweetheart," I breathe against her neck, sucking and biting the sweet spot on her collarbone. She gasps, hands clutching the back of my head as my lips kiss down the front of her body, tongue laving the pebbled peaks practically poking holes through my shirt.

Setting her down, my hands at her waist, "We'll get to this later. Every summer night I'm going to feast on you until you scream my name in your head so loud it' will leave a scar in your brain. You won't be able to think about sex or look at your naked body in the mirror without seeing my hands on you and feeling me here." I reach down cupping her mound hard.

Her hands grip me to keep from falling over. "I've always been a good girl. But you make me want to be so bad."

Stroking my hand slowly back and forth, I watch hypnotized as her eyes shut. "You'll be my good girl. *Just mine, Callie.*"

"Yes." She moans, hips riding my hand. It feels so fucking good, commanding her body like this. But I need to stop.

"No."

"No? Why?"

"Do you need this baby?"

"I do, so much. Please," she whispers.

Taking her mouth with mine, my hand slides down the soaked T-shirt skirts the hem and slips under. Finding the edge of her panties, my fingers jerk it aside, to run along her lips, spread them and find the pearl nestled inside.

"You're so wet. So, fucking wet for me, Callie. You want me to let you come?"

"Do it. Please." Her eyes flutter open, raw with need. My jaw ticks, I won't deny her what she needs despite the nights I've denied myself.

My fingers toy with her; drawing it out—making her pant hot little sweet breaths of need against my lips.

My head lowers tongue sucking her nipple through the molded fabric on her skin. I won't risk any early morning joggers seeing my girl, but damn, do I want to taste her bare tits again.

My dick's so hard despite the cold swirling surf. We're both burning up, even though the sun's rays have just barely peaked over the horizon.

Quickening the pace, my fingers slide and swirl, pinch and twist her needy clit until she comes in my hand in a rush of throaty moans and jerking hips.

Withdrawing, I carry her out of the water, placing her down in the sand.

"I'll see you later, baby. I'm taking you out tonight."

She smiles drowsily, still coming down from the orgasm that ripped through her.

"I'll pick you up at 6:30." My hands grab her face for a quick kiss before they reluctantly drop. Turning back down the beach to finish my workout, I look over my shoulder at her feeling more of a champion then I did when we won the Rose Bowl sophomore year. She sinks in the sand on rubbery legs, sated and craving more, *of me*.

When I'm out of sight, my hands fist pump in the air. This girl has wit, brains, a body that keeps me up at night, and tonight *she's all mine*.

FIFTEEN

CALLIE

"HEY CALLIE," SOPHIE CALLS out as I enter the café forty minutes late.

She looks me over and puts a hand over her mouth, "You saw him, didn't you?"

I nod, moving behind the counter to put my apron on. "So?"

"He's... he's ... I can't even explain it."

"I knew it."

"Knew what?"

"That he's what you need. You've been working your ass like a single mom whose husband left her a pile of debt, instead of a college girl home for summer."

"Um... I'm always home for summer, Soph. I live at home, remember?"

"It's an expression." She gestures with the coffee pot in hand.

"My stomach clenches every time I think about how he touched me. This thing between us is like nothing I've ever dared to dream about. He not only keeps me on my toes—he melts them."

"And that's why I called Banger and told them who you were."

"I figured as much when he showed up at my house this morning."

"Oh? That's a good excuse for the boss to be late."

Face on fire; I pick up a stack of menus walking over to the couple who just entered. Ignoring Soph's knowing grin for the next half hour, I keep myself busy, too busy to think of his smoldering eyes and even hotter body until the buzz from my cell vibrates in my back pocket.

My New Hot Boyfriend: I still taste you on my tongue.

Blushing I type back,

Who is this?

My New Hot Boyfriend: Do I need to come to the café and remind you?

Breath short, butterflies flying in my tummy, I type back.

I DARE YOU.

My New Hot Boyfriend: I'm placing my lunch order. *You*—*w*ith a side of fries.

My eyes flit over to the clock my grand poppy hung when he opened this café forty years ago. Grinning my fingers tap out,

Fries aren't on the menu. How did you get my number?

My New Hot Boyfriend: Swiped it from your back patio while you recovered from... me on the beach. You really should lock your phone. Especially if you're going to text Soph how hot I am and how good my hands are.

. . .

"Oh, my God!" Mortified, I know I need to clear out fast before he catches me.

Untying my waitressing apron from around my waist, I type one last order into the computer for the cooks to read. I ordered him a surf and turf salad, crab cakes and a deluxe order of sweet potatoes fries. I cash out the order, using my tip money to pay for his lunch.

Taking a pen and a blank sheet of paper from my ordering pad I write:

With a grin, I call Sophie over. "When he comes in serve him the food from ticket number twenty-nine and hand him this.

She reads the note shaking her head. "I need a summer romance like this."

"I thought you were done with summer boys."

"There is someone, but he doesn't see me when he's too busy staring at someone else."

"I'm sorry."

"Don't be. I'm fine. Now go before he gets here."

Strapping on my fanny pack, unlocking my bike, I pedal hard against traffic down to the docks thinking I love being chased just as much as he loves trying to catch me.

SIXTEEN

GABE

I SPENT MOST OF THE day planning our date. A girl like Callie needs to be impressed. Somehow, I doubt, fancy restaurants, fast cars, and smooth talking are her thing.

Between my Waze app and Banger's help: I'm hoping to put stars in her eyes by the end of the night. The woman has my heart doing flips, my mind planning a million things I shouldn't and my dick ready to blow like Mt. Vesuvius.

I cleaned up the beach cottage just in case we ended up here later. Not that it needed much. But I stocked my fridge with wine and cheese, put fresh flowers out in one of the many glass vases I found and changed my sheets—just in case. I even had time to put my car through the wash and vacuum it out. To say this girl affects me is an understatement.

Taking one last look around, I check everything I packed with a grin.

My phone lights up. Jackie? Again?! Ignoring her; I put my phone down.

It rings for a second time.

Dad Cell.

Ignoring him too, I hop in my car and get ready for the first date that will end all others.

She's done.

Mine.

Period.

Just as I'm turning down her street my phone rings again: **Coach**.

I debate answering, but Callie is the only thing on my mind. Putting my car in park, I turn my phone off sliding into my pocket.

She's already outside. In the same spot, I found her twelve hours earlier. She looks fucking beautiful—heart-stopping beautiful. Her long chocolate-colored locks fly in the wind.

She's wearing white.

I feel the tick in my cheek. The primal need to mate with her, claim her in the most basic way is replaced with something sweeter than her lips; the image of her in a gown walking towards me.

Christ, I need to slow this train down. It's only our first date, and yet... I already see our future. Which is completely crazy since I don't believe in love at first sight or any of that shit.

But then again, how else can I explain the mess of things I'm feeling?

She turns sensing me staring at her like a predator.

"Hey!"

She jumps down from the sea wall, and my eyes can't help dropping to her tanned legs. But her white summer dress and cute sandals won't do.

"Hey. You look stunning, but you'll need to change."

"Oh, yeah?"

"Oh, yeah. I have an exceptional first date planned. Something so spectacular you'll never forget it. Tell your parents you might not be home until after three."

"Three? Umm, no. I need to be at the café at five forty-five am."

"Oh, okay. In that case... tell them you're not coming home at all."

Her eyebrows reach her hairline. "Okay... let me call Sophie in case you actually are some wacko human trafficker or something."

"That's the furthest thing from who I am. You didn't try to find me on social media?"

"No. I hate Facebook. I don't Tweet. McWow is for perverts or serial killers, but I will warn you—I have a serious Pinterest addiction."

"Noted."

I knew she was fucking perfect. She's not one of those chicks whose face is always glued to her phone or taking selfies after fluffing their hair for fifteen minutes.

"Come on," she gestures standing in the door motioning me to follow, "help me pick out something to wear for this epic date you planned."

"Well, if I get to choose... you'll end up in a bikini all night," I laugh coming up behind her hugging her waist. "I've missed you," I mumble against her hair, kissing the back of her neck.

"It's only been half a day."

"Half-a-day too long."

"How can you miss someone you barely even know?"

"Babe, I've been missing you for years."

She practically melts against me. But for once, I'm not playing, feeding her lines—I mean every word.

She takes my hand leading me through modern, airy rooms, up the stairs opening a door at the end of the hall.

"Where's your family? I'd like to meet them."

"They're not here for the summer. It's just me." She spoke softly, hurt flashing in her eyes.

"Callie?"

"It's not a story for a first date. I want to have fun tonight. Can we just do that?"

"I'm the king of fun."

"I bet you are."

My eyes sweep her room. It's just as fresh and clean as the woman who sleeps in it. The walls are painted a faint pink. Her furniture's all white with rose gold and black touches splash color placed here and there. The rose I plucked this morning sits in a vase on her dresser. "Did you hire an interior designer?"

"No. I told you I'm a Pinterest junkie."

"I'm impressed."

"So?" She gestures for me to walk towards her closet.

My hand touches her clothing, moves a hanger....it feels more intimate than anything we've shared.

She watches, crossing her arms waiting to see what I'll pick. I find a pair of those skinny jeans all the girls wear, a thick hooded sweatshirt, hiking boots, and walk past her to her bed where I scoop up a stuffed cheetah.

"He can come too," I smirk.

"Don't make fun of Thor. He was a gift from my baby brother."

She snatches it from my hands putting him carefully back.

"What's his name?"

"Charlie. He's five. He's with my dad—," she stops, obviously trying not to cry. Figuring her parents are probably divorced. I drop it.

"Hey, it's okay. I'm sorry."

"No. I'm sorry. I just miss them."

I nod my head, hands still full of her clothes. "Oh, you might want to bring a bathing suit... just in case."

"Ok. I'll be right out." Taking her clothes, she kisses me on the cheek, walks into a small bathroom, not in the least fazed by the outfit I selected.

Tonight is going to be perfect.

I could get used to the way she's looking at me. It's obvious I caught her by surprise when I drove in the opposite direction from town, turning into the state park.

"We're going hiking?"

"For starters." Lifting the back gate of my SUV, I take out a wicker hamper and a thick plaid blanket. "I thought we'd hike up to the cliffs catch the sunset, go to dinner, then maybe walk down the beach. There's a meteor shower tonight. But it starts after midnight. I'll understand if you're too tired, though."

"No. Stargazing with you sounds incredible."

My shoulders relax as I take her hand. We walk in comfortable silence taking in the scenery as we go. The sun's still warm as we reach the trail leading up the cliff. The sand is packed hard mixed with rocks and dirt. Hand in hand; we help each other climb until we reach the top.

"I've always loved this spot. My parents used to take me hiking here."

Placing our things down, my arms reach around her waist as we watch the sun lower. "Tell me about them?" My lips kiss her shoulder. She sighs leaning back into my embrace. "They're still so in love. It's incredible but at times incredibly sad."

She pauses, so I wait for her to continue.

"My mom's sick. She has stage three leukemia. The doctors put her chance of survival at forty percent."

"Callie...," I whisper pulling her closer.

"My dad...we rented an apartment next to the hospital at

UVA, so he could be closer, now that Charlie's school year is done. I-I had to stay behind to run things..."

"We don't have to talk about it." I can tell she's getting upset.

"No. I want to. I want you to understand why meeting you set something off inside me. You brought laughter back in my life, ignited my inner streak of rebellion that I've forgotten about. In a way—you jump-started my heart."

I spin her around in my arms, "Callie," I breath against her lips wishing I could kiss every pain away, "if I started yours— you stopped mine."

"I'm not good at this."

"At what, baby?" My face nuzzles her hair, smelling of lavender and sunscreen.

"Romance."

"Oh yeah? Well, I've got that covered."

Wanting to take her mind off her troubles, I spread the blanket down, taking out a cold bottle of wine.

She sits next to me, hesitating. "I don't drink."

"Great." Without missing a beat, I reach for the chilled seltzer water instead. "I'm in pre-season. I'm not drinking either."

"Pre-season?"

"Yeah. I guess I should tell you...I'm not a serial killer, but I am a wanted man."

Sighing, my eyes search the horizon. "I came to Sea Spray to hide. I'm kind of a big deal. You don't watch football, do you?"

She shakes her head. "What are you, UVA's star quarterback or something?"

"Or something." Taking a sip of my drink, my eyes find hers. "I'm the lead wide receiver. I've scored more touch downs than anyone else in the college football. I hold the record."

"That's how."

My eyebrows rise.

"...you caught me that night. You were so far out in the water and then in seconds... you had me."

Heat curls inside my stomach, abs clenching as I remember the feel of her soft body imprinted against mine. I can't wait to feel her under me again, but next time, hopefully well be naked. "I've never been faster. Training here has re-invigorated me. There are no distractions. At first, I thought it was the sea air, but it's you. You, Callie, are doing wild things to me."

A blush blooms on her cheek, the same color as the rose I picked.

"What are you hiding from Parker?"

"It's Gabe. My full name is Gabe Parker." I wait for the recognition to come, but it never does. Instead, her face holds a sweet expression with soft eyes full of trust.

"Callie." My hand reaches for hers across the blanket. "That night we first met, and I begged you not to call the police on me... that was the same night the press chased me out of UVA. I was in the crosshairs of a cheating scandal. I'm innocent, but I can't say all the other athletes are. It's bad. The College is not the only ones investigating, but the NCAA and a private inquiry has been launched by the national association of state colleges."

"I heard something about it at the café. People were talking about a scandal at UVA that involved athletes, but I tuned most of it out. I'm glad I heard it first hand from you though."

My hand rubs the back of my neck. "This is one heck of a first date, huh?"

Her lips part. "It's real though. There's no pretending we're two perfect people. Living two perfect lives and trying to impress one another with how great we are."

"Oh, I'm great baby. Don't doubt that," I wink.

"I wish we could stay up here forever. Suspended with the clouds, locked in time. All our problems on pause."

"Me, too." I lay back on one elbow, my forefinger rubbing the soft inside of her wrist. "I was dating a girl named Jackie last year. She pretended to be someone she isn't and didn't take it well when I ended our relationship." I pause, looking her in the eyes wondering how I ever dated Jackie as long as I did.

"Anyway... she showed up late to my apartment one night, totally blitzed out of her mind... screaming. She was waking up my neighbors. Truthfully—I couldn't let her leave in the state she was in. She could've gotten herself into trouble. We ended up driving around campus all night while she alternated between screaming, crying, and hitting me. I was so angry that I wasted almost two years with her—I told her I'd never put a ring on her finger... that I never loved her, because I didn't."

"Why did you date her for so long then?"

"Shit. I'm going to sound like an asshole—she was convenient. She cooked for me, hung out while everyone else partied, and kept my bed warm. But I was never thinking long-term. We never clicked... like you and I do. There was never even a fraction of the spark I feel every time I touch you."

She sucks in a breath as my hand slides up her arm trailing back down.

"Anyway, I finally dropped her off at her dorm, where she refused to get out of my car. I literally dumped her at the curb driving straight to my Calculus exam where I flunked—miserably. My coach somehow convinced my professor to give me a make-up a week later. I almost passed that, *perfectly*. My professor found that to be suspicious and sounded the alarm. Coincidentally, it came to light—one of the TA's was screwing the point guard on the basketball team. She was giving him all the exams in advance all semester. He was selling them for a hundred bucks a piece.

I'm being roped into all this shit despite not doing a damn thing."

"Why? Why are they targeting you? Can't that ball player just admit he never sold you a copy of the exam?"

"I wish it were that simple. He lawyered up. His scholarship and shot at the NBA are on the line. It came out that the TA wasn't the only woman on campus he was messing around with. She's pissed. She kept texts of their exchanges talking about the exams. There's a full-blown investigation by the NCAA and the University. I re-took an exam last week in front of them all. Aced that mother fucker, too. I'm hoping that proves I'm clear of this—but until then I'm laying low—here with you."

Sitting up, I haul her into my lap, kiss her sweet lips, not waiting another second to get my hands on her. She pulls back, mind working, "why do they want you if it was the basketball team that cheated?"

Sighing, my hands cup up to cup her cheek. "Because Callie, I could've gone pro, entered the draft this past spring. But I didn't. I have the most completed catches in the end zone in college football—ever. I'm even more popular than the quarterback. ESPN has reporters all over campus looking for me."

Callie's phone rings interrupting me, but she ignores the call. Then it rings for a second and third time.

"I'm sorry. I need to take this in case it's an emergency... Soph? Is everything, okay?" Her eyes cut to mine, my fists clench knowing it's nothing good.

She sighs hands falling to her sides. "That was my best friend, Sophie..."

I nod.

"It's bad, Gabe. Your ex talked to the press and is giving Entertainment Tonight an exclusive interview. She's all over social media, TMZ, and Perez Hilton."

"Christ."

"There's more. She says that she's having your baby."

"WHAT?" I roar. "That scheming bitch. I swear to you, Callie. I haven't been with her in months." Springing to my feet, I stalk to the edge of the cliff.

"Unless that's how far along—"

"No! I just saw her on campus. She was waiting by my car. She's not pregnant—she's full of shit."

Her small arms wrap around me, "I believe you."

Those three words mean everything. I'm finally here with her...I'm not going to lose my chance because of bullshit lies.

Her head rests against my back, my arms come up over hers, linking our hands, I bring one of hers to my mouth. We watch the sun fade in silence until I turn to face her. "I need to check my phone."

"I knew this moment was too good to last."

"I promise you, Callie. Once I get through this—we'll have a million moments like this."

Fifty new voicemails and a hundred texts greet me. Each more panicked than the last, well except the one from my father threatening me. If I lose my scholarship, I'm done. He won't help pay for my senior year at UVA, which is just fine because I wouldn't take a dime anyway. He can suck my nutsack when I'm in the pro's.

Out of all of the people that called, I return the only call that matters.

"Coach."

"Parker. I can't protect you this time. Personal shit is out of my control."

"I understand sir. What about the investigation?"

"You were clear. But Jackie's story... could change things."

"What? Why? If she's pregnant, it's not mine."

"She said you cheated, son. All four years, not just in the classroom but on the field."

"BULLSHIT! You know I'm clean."

"It looks bad. Scandal after scandal. The NCAA wants all your medical records, and you need to report back here for supervised drug testing."

"This isn't fair. I'm innocent."

"I know, son. I know. Just keep your head down. I'm doing everything I can. But Gabe—the NFL doesn't want any more bad press after the year they had. If you get cleared—"

"When I get cleared."

"... you are going to need to have one hell of a season to get picked early in the draft."

"Fucking hell."

"I'll be in touch."

"Gabe?" Callie grabs my hand, squeezing it.

"Can we just... have the date I planned? Let the world fall away until tomorrow, please?"

She nods, arms going around my waist. My head rests on top of hers, closing my eyes, savoring the feeling of having this girl in my arms after weeks of thinking about her. I just hope she stays.

After the hike, I took her back here, not wanting to risk someone recognizing me at one of the restaurants in town now that my face is once again plastered everywhere. I cooked her shrimp scampi with pasta. I even indulged in a glass of chilled Chardonnay. We talked about everything—our childhood—our parents, what we have in common. I want to know everything about her. Become a part of her story—maybe we'll even write ours complete with a ride into the sunset in a friggin' horse-drawn carriage. She makes me feel that kind of fairytale shit.

I haven't seen so many stars since the hit I took freshman year from Cal Harrison at Ole Miss.

I'm fucked.

No matter what happens, I want to hang on to this one. My hands squirt dish soap onto the plates. I give them a good rinse before placing them in the washer. She wanted to help clear up, but I wouldn't hear of it. Especially when she told me the situation with her mom, leaving her to run two businesses all day.

"Callie? You want dessert, baby?"

Silence.

Turning off the faucet, my bare feet are quiet as I walk back out to the small den.

She's asleep.

Curled up on the couch like an angel. Her long dark locks fall all around her. Soft pink lips are parted, cheeks flushed as she breathes deeply in and out. It feels like someone just reached into my chest and put their hands around my heart, squeezing so hard I can't breathe.

Grabbing the light quilted blanket, I wrap her in it lift her in my arms and carry her outside. She mumbles something incoherent against my neck as I sit in the sand watching the sky.

With her in my arms, I have everything I need to face the storm coming. Cradling her like a baby, my hands and lips find her face and her hair. "Gabe?" Her eyes slowly blink.

"Shhh, go back to sleep. I like holding you."

"Did I miss the star shower?"

"No. We have thirty minutes."

"How are we going to kill time?"

Feeling a stupid grin light up my face, my hand brings her face closer.

"... hmmm... I could think of a few ways..."

My lips take hers as my hands unwrap the blanket. In one motion I lay her down, coming on top. Resting my weight on my elbows, I groan into her mouth as her legs spread, letting me rest my thick cock in between.

Her hands roam up under my shirt, kneading the knots in my back. A hiss tears from me as her nails lightly rake up my abs then down my happy trail. She cups me boldly, hands sliding up and down.

"That feels so good baby," I murmur moving away from her mouth to lift her shirt over her head.

My dick twerks.

That's right twerks at the sight of her dusky nipples playing peek-a-boo through her ivory lace bra.

My tongue slides over them, trying to poke holes in the lace as my lips tug both fabric and breast into my starving mouth.

She moves beneath me, seeking relief running her hands through my hair. Unclasping her bra, I feel the pre-cum oozing out of me as my eyes feast on her... again.

Lowering my head to those sweet tips, my mouth pays each the attention they deserve. I hiss as her soft hands find my hard length stroking up and down.

Rearing back, I slip my shorts off needing to be closer her.

My fingers hesitate at the zipper on her shorts. "Callie?"

She nods her consent; my fingers shake as I remove another layer of clothing, getting closer to glory.

She's bathed in moonlight and stars. Her nipples are wet from my mouth; my eyes take in her slit barely covered by a lace thong. She hesitates, attempting to cover herself.

"There's no one here. This small strip of beach behind the house is private. Let me in?"

Biting her lip, she answers. "Can we just make out? I-I'm not... the last time I did this, it didn't feel so good."

My head snaps back, anger and jealousy mixing a deadly potion. "You're mine. No one else's—I promise you, Callie. It's going to feel fucking divine when this happens. But I'll wait. I'm playing the long game."

Coming back on top of my goddess, my hands and mouth touch her everywhere. She's lost in us. Just like me.

My fingers sneak inside the scrappy lace; I almost come in my pants at the feel of her smooth mound and soaked hot folds —imagining what it would be like to enter her bare. I play with her clit, circling the swollen pearl, round and round before darting away and penetrating her with two fingers. Curling them up, I rub her G-spot watching her face as she loses all control.

My lips take hers prisoner, as my hands stay between her legs, stroking, rubbing, finger-fucking her good.

"Gabe!" She moans coming on my fingers.

"Fuck!" I groan withdrawing my hand. Letting my hard as fuck cock press up against her dripping pussy through my boxer briefs.

"Babe. I promise I won't, but I need to imagine I'm inside you."

She answers by pulling me back down to her. My hips come between her legs; I hook one around me—panties still jerked aside, the tip of my dick only covered by a thin layer of cotton, parts her.

Her wet heat soaks through.

I go in three inches, backing out using my briefs a shield. Her hot breath puffs in my ear as my dick presses on her clit. I dry hump the shit out of her blowing my load like a teen getting the tip of his dick wet for the first time. It was better than fucking a million girls raw. The force of my orgasm leaves me weak. Falling next to her, I laugh seeing shooting stars in the sky.

"I see them too. But the ones, I saw in your embrace were better."

My load's leaking everywhere. Winking at her, I strip. "Feel like a midnight swim?"

She stands wearing only her thong and takes my hand.

"Best first date ever," I grin as we jog into the surf washing each other clean.

Callie

Tan forearms corded with strong muscles hold me close. My eyes drop to them wrapped around my pale waist. His thick cock presses insistently against my butt.

"Morning, babe."

Reaching out, I turn the alarm on my phone off. It's still not quite light out. We've only slept for four hours but the orgasms he gave helped me sleep deeply.

"Morning," I mumble feeling shy.

Gabe walked me home never letting go of my hand. He looked at me with soft eyes that begged to stay. Truthfully, I'm so addicted I didn't want him to leave. He held me all night, kissed the back of my neck, breathed in my hair like I'm the most precious thing in the world to him. I feel cherished, and it's making my heart all giddy.

"Mmmmm, sleep in with me." He asks as I reluctantly wiggle free. His arms catch me, pulling me right back where I was. One hand dips low, cupping me, the other massages my breast.

"Horny beast!"

"Only for you my beauty." His fingers play with me as he

nudges his dick between my ass cheeks.

"Gabe... I'm not—not very experienced. Like at all."

He slows his ministrations but doesn't stop.

"Like how inexperienced?"

"I've only had sex once. *It was a total disaster.*"

"I wish you had waited... *for me.*"

My heart stops beating. He's so fucking romantic, and I've already lost all the walls I had around my heart. He crumpled the last of them last night.

His hand stops playing, palm pressing flat against me—hard. "I'll always take care of you, babe. In and out of the bedroom. I'm in no rush. Just promise me—*this is mine.*"

"Yes!" I gasp as he takes his hot cock out, resting it on my ass. I feel a few drops fall from him, trickling down my skin.

He grunts, carefully sliding himself between my pressed legs so he can snuggle up against the lips of my pussy.

"I'm your man, babe." He pulls a hand from my legs to touch the tip of his dick. I almost come at how kinky he is as he coats the tips of my nipples with his pre-cum.

"There. I want you wearing me all day."

His hand drops back down, and neither of us speak as his fingers swirl through me, up me, as his dick glides between my thighs using my own wetness to slide back and forth.

He stops, taking himself in his hand and leans over me—spilling hot come all over my tan tummy.

I watch, mesmerized at how sexy he is, eyes burning for me as he comes, watching himself spurt all over me. Some splashing up on my breasts. His dick jerks more, he bites his lip, moaning my name.

I feel powerful knowing this God of a man is so hot for me. Quickly kneeling, my mouth catches the last drops; his dick jerk in my mouth.

"God, Callie. That was hot!"

His hand rubs between my thighs, pressing my clit, I straddle his thigh, rubbing against it like a bitch in heat. I've never discovered this side of me before. I feel liberated. Like I can be his sexy dirty girlfriend without shame because he makes me forget everything but the need to be with him like this.

We stare at each other with matching flushed cheeks, dirty sex hands, blended sweat, and hearts. He's the first to recover, taking me by the hand and leading me into my own shower, where he tenderly rinses me while peppering my shoulders and back with quick kisses.

The man can't keep his bear paw hands off me—I hope he never stops putting them on me.

"Someone's chipper this morning. I texted all night wondering what the brawny footballer was doing to you."

"He did—just about everything but carry me off in a pirate ship with my wrists bound."

"Damn that would be hot."

"Don't give me any ideas."

We both jump at his deep voice right behind us.

"Gabe?"

"Hey, babe." He gives Soph a wink as I'm pulled back into his strong arms. My eyes flutter shut, savoring the feel of him holding me as the smell of his spicy cologne surrounds me.

"What are you doing here?" My voice sounds breathless. A slow burn runs up my body landing on my cheeks. I'm embarrassed by the intimacy we shared now that he's here in broad daylight.

"Hi, I'm Sophie."

Gabe lifts one hand off my waist to shake hers.

"Uh, the two of you better go out back. People are staring."

"Shit." Gabe breathes taking my hand and leading me through the open back door.

"GABE! OVER HERE! IS IT TRUE YOU MIGHT BE BENCHED?"

"GABE! Have you heard from the NCAA regarding your eligibility?"

"From Dirty player to BABY DADDY! Is she keeping the baby?"

The clicks of the camera's are followed by flashes. The shouts accompany the sound of furniture being pushed out of the way.

Stopping short, Gabe shields me with his body as a group of reporters crowd us on the beach behind the café.

I try to turn around, but more are behind us.

"How did they find me?" He mutters. My hands skim up and down his arm trying to soothe the flexed muscles.

"Callie? Did you—"

"No. Of course, not. I haven't breathed a word to anyone about you."

His lips are thin as he weighs our options. "Stay close."

He uses his giant body and broad shoulders to fight through the frantic crowd. With my head hanging low, one hand tucked tightly in his, the other shielding my face, he follows Sophie's shout of "over here!"

We find safety in the back office of the café where I bolt the door.

He sighs, running a hand through his hair. "I'm sorry. I had hoped we'd have more time before... all of this started." He gestures with his hand, frustration written all over his face.

"It's—wow—I've never experienced anything like that."

"It might get worse. Can you—will you stick with me?"

"Like glue."

He smiles relieved I'm not running from this despite the shitshow his life's becoming.

He sighs, taking me in his arms, holding me close. "I need you, babe. It'd take a Trojan army to try to take you away from me. But I wouldn't go down like Troy. I'd slay every last one to get to you."

"You're such a romantic for a big jock."

"Did you hear?"

"Hear what?"

"The angels crying when I stole you from heaven?"

Smacking his arm, I giggle, "if you used that line on me. I would've walked."

"No, you wouldn't have. I saw stars in your eyes every time you looked at me."

"Cocky jock."

"Guilty." He leans down kissing me sweetly. "I need to go. I have a meeting on campus with my coach and the athletic director. I might not be back until late tonight. Callie—I might need a lawyer. I'm not going to stand for Jackie's smear campaign. I'm going to hit back—hard and sue her for slander and damages."

"Damages?"

"If she fucks me and I get benched kicked off the team and lose my shot at the NFL—they'll be damages. Can I drive you to the marina? You can't bike over with vans full of paparazzi on your tail. One of them could hit you."

"Yeah, that's probably a good idea."

We both laugh at the sight of my fanny pack on the desk. "Are you ready? We're going to have to sprint to my car."

"Wait." Grabbing his head pulling it to mine, my lips find his, "now, I'm ready."

He pauses at the door, eyes finding mine. "I already miss you."

"Well, come find me later."

"You know I will."

SEVENTEEN

GABE

THE DRIVE TO CAMPUS WENT in a blur of remembering my time with Callie; how her breasts tasted under the stars... the way she moaned in my ear as her hips moved under me, and the way I shuddered when her hands wrapped around my cock.

It's only been three weeks since the night we met, but she's already under my skin, in my blood, making my heart her next home.

My ball cap's pulled low as I eye a place to park where I can dodge the press milling relentlessly around.

I give up, deciding to park in one of the empty lots behind the dorm I stayed in freshman year. It's close enough to the field house and has a path that cuts through the woods to the athletic complex.

Taking a deep breath, I get out knowing whatever happens today could change the direction my life's going.

No one's around, my feet jog through the path, down the hill and I use my fob key to enter a backdoor of the athletic complex before anyone can spot me. Heading down familiar halls, it's not long before I'm once again knocking on Coach's door.

"Parker."

Déjà vu hits me as he sits, eyes glued to the monitor of his computer. His face is red—all the way to his hairline.

"Sir?"

"SIT!"

What the fuck?

He finally tears his eyes away from whatever was so riveting on his screen to give me a dressing down.

"Was I not clear that you were to lay low? Train—get your head right and stay away from girls?"

"I've never been in better shape, Coach. I'm in every night, up before dawn to get my work out in and been to work on time every shift."

"Uh-huh. Spare me the crap." He turns the screen towards me.

Motherfucker.

My hand comes up to rub my face, half hoping it'd be gone when I look at it again.

It's not.

Some fuck captured Callie in my arms on the beach last night and topless in the waves as I grinned down at her like a lovesick fool.

"I'm falling in love with her, Sir."

His palm smacks the desk.

"Like hell you are. Dammit, I should've known a jock like you wouldn't be able to resist the summer girl by the shore."

"She's not a summer girl," I grate out through clenched teeth.

"Looks that way to me."

He scrolls down, my knees bounce, fists ready to land blows

as image after image of Callie naked in my arms in the sand and sea stare back at me.

"Where is this?"

"TMZ, Perez Hilton, and a few others... Pop Sugar? At least US Weekly blacked out her lady bits."

My head drops in my hands. I'm choking on rage and the need to punch a hole through the wall. My girl. My sweet, shy girl—should never have been humiliated this way.

"Call a press conference. Let them come at me. This shit with her ends—now!"

"Slow down. The NCAA is here. You're being drug tested." He slides a small plastic cup across the desk, prelabeled with my name and date on it.

"They want a blood sample, too."

"My life's being turned-upside-down."

"Just wait until the NFL. This is pre-school."

My head snaps back. He's right. I just want to play the game, always did. But all the shit that comes with it at this level and the next—is sucking all the joy from the sport I've loved since my hand fit around the pigskin laces.

"Coach—I... there was no one there."

"You have a lot to learn about the business side of the game, son. They had cameras probably out on a boat with those zoom lenses that can snap a gnat on your sleeve from a mile away."

"Fuck."

"Exactly."

"I gotta call her."

He nods his head. "Ten-minutes. That's all you get. Put your personal life aside because we have your future career to save."

He shuts the door as he leaves. I get up pacing the small office like a caged animal, hyped up and wanting to tear into something.

"Callie."

Our calls connected but she doesn't speak.

"Babe—I'm sorry."

"Sorry? I'm beyond embarrassed. They figured out who the topless girl on the beach was after we were spotted together this morning. My—my uncle is the chief of police. He had to walk into the station with all his beat cops looking at my tits on their phones." She breaks off choking on the tears I can imagine are pouring from my angel's eyes.

It's tearing me up, and I can't do a damn thing to make this right.

"Fuck, baby. It's killing me that they hurt you like this..."

"I—can't Gabe. My father's calling."

"I'll see you tonight. I just want to hold you."

"I—I don' t think that's a good idea..."

"I thought you said you were done running."

"That was before—before I ended up 'the dirty player's dirty little secret', right next to a picture of your ex, claiming she's having your child."

"Callie..."

But she's gone.

Ended the call.

Leaving me behind again.

EIGHTEEN
CALLIE

"CALLIE?"

"Oh, Mom!"

I hesitate in the doorway. She wasn't expecting me. But sometimes you just need your mother and having your face and naked body splashed all over the tabloids definitely qualifies.

"Oh, honey come here."

My lip quivers, hair's a tangled mess, clothes wrinkled as I enter the room.

"You look worse than me."

Sinking down in a chair next to the bed, I lay my head on her lap. She strokes my hair just as she has so many times before when I needed it.

"Where's Dad and Charlie?"

"They went out for ice cream."

"How pissed is Dad?"

She doesn't answer, so I raise my head.

"Mom?"

Her finger presses the button on her hospital bed raising it so that she can sit up. IV's connected to bags run from her wrist. My finger touches the hospital band she's worn like a bracelet for months.

"Callie... I—I want you to *live*. And from the way your eyes looked at that boy, you are. Don't stop. Don't stop falling in love even if it hurts like nothing else. The journey will be worth it."

"You saw the pictures?"

"I did. It made me feel better than the pain meds. I was up early watching the news and there you were with Gabe Parker outside The Blue Hydrangea. Then well... they showed the pictures the paparazzi snapped but don't worry sweeties, they blurred—"

My face falls into my hands. "Did Dad—"

"Yes. I told him to go cool off. And reminded him we were both your age once and did the same things."

"I didn't need to hear that."

"Sorry. I know we put a lot on your shoulders. It hurts me so much that you're carrying our burdens."

"I just want you to be okay, Mom. That's all I care about. Besides, I love the café and the marina. It's part of my blood now too."

She pats my hand. "I know. But I want you to be a doctor like you dream of being. You can always come back for visits, but I want more for you than to pour coffee and clear tables.

"I will. Don't you worry. My summer classes started, but how can I show my face now?" I groan.

"It'll pass, you'll see."

I don't want to upset her in her fragile state, so I pretend she's right. But there's no way this will die down, especially in Sea Spray where the only thing exciting that ever happens is when a shark is spotted close to shore.

"So how are you really doing, Mom? I'm not a kid like Charlie. I deserve to know."

"Better. Truly. I'm just weak. They said—they said I might need a bone marrow transplant."

"Fine. I'm here test me."

She looks away, fingers brushing mine. "Mom?"

"We already found a match. It's... Charlie. But—I'll never put him through that. He's too young."

"You have to Mom. Please! We both need you to beat this. He'll never forgive you when he's older if you don't let him give you the chance to live."

Her eyes snap back to mine. "You're wiser than your years. I... I never thought of it like that."

"I'll tell the doctors. Let's not wait."

"No. he's my baby boy, so young and sweet. *I can't.* Not yet. I've decided to let this chemo treatment run its course and go from there."

"I'm so scared. I don't think we should chance anything."

She's about to reply when a nurse in bright pink scrubs scurries in, screeching to a halt seeing me. Her cheeks quickly match her shirt as she finds the remote turning on the TV.

My gasp echoes as Gabe's face fills the screen.

It's surreal.

Weird.

Hot AF—seeing him dressed in a crisp white shirt and sports coat. His tan face, somber as he faces the cameras. His dark hair glistens, but his eyes are hard. He's sitting at a press conference with the University's banner hanging behind him.

I melt.

He's mine for the taking. All I have to do is surrender the rest of my body. I want him. I do. But I'm terrified my heart and soul won't survive sex after him. He probably fucks like a champ as well.

My face heats as his eyes stare right through the screen finding mine.

Three pairs of riveted eyes watch and wait for him to speak.

"First off, I want to let Coach, the Athletic Director, my team and my fans how very grateful I am for your support during this trying time.

I've never cheated on or off the field... or taken any performing enhancing drugs. A few days ago, I sat in a room with the President of UVA, the Chancellor, my professor and my coach. I sat and took a Calc exam prepared just for me. It was delivered in a locked briefcase, graded in front of everyone and put back in that locked briefcase—" He pauses, eyes hard, enunciating every word. "I didn't just pass. I scored a ninety-six. I am also 100% going to pass any drug testing today or in the future. As for my personal life—my attorney will be serving a subpoena to Jackie Delaware for a court-ordered pregnancy test. I am also suing her for defamation, slander, and damages resulting in her false statements she has made about me."

My hands twist the end of my mother's bed sheets.

"That boy is on fire. Damn, um-hum. That girl's going to regret spewing lies about him." The nurse clucks, hands on her plump hips.

Camera's flash as he sits back in his seat, reporters rapid firing questions.

"GABE! WHO is your new girl?"
"IS IT SERIOUS?"
"WILL YOU BE LIVING IN SEA SPRAY?"

His jaw clenched he leans forward into the microphone, holding a hand up for silence. "Vultures," he spits, index finger digging into the table, "so much for you being here for the game. For wanting to know that the integrity of this University is high and so is their athletic department."

The other men at the table straighten, pleased that Gabe stood up for them.

His coach takes questions; I can tell it's taking Gabe everything not to stand up and walk.

My eyes swing to the door as Dad and Charlie come in!

"Hey, Char!" My arms go wide as he flings himself on me. I bury my nose in his hair, closing my eyes—I missed him so much.

"Let's go Callie girl."

Reluctantly, my eyes open finding Dad's.

"Where?"

"Lunch."

"But you just had ice cream."

He purses his lips giving me the 'Dad look,' I haven't seen since senior year when Sophie and I snuck out and threw a boat party.

"I'll see you later bud."

"But you just got here."

"I know... maybe you could come home this weekend? We can boogie board and go mini golfing?"

"I don't think that's a good idea."

"Why not?" My hurt eyes meet my father's.

"Your uncle called. Our house is surrounded by news trucks."

"This isn't happening. This isn't my life."

"It is if you want to date Gabe Parker," Dad mutters.

"You don't approve?"

He's silent, eyes studying me. "Lunch. I'm starving."

"I'll be back," I kiss Charlie on the cheek, following Dad out the door. I glance over my shoulder at Charlie snuggled up to Mom's side. She changed the channel to the Cartoon

Network. He's tired after being at camp all morning and his eyes start to drop.

He can't lose her. He's barely a fifth of my age.

I need to look out for my baby brother and make sure he doesn't.

"Dad—we can't just sit by and let her call the shots anymore." We walk down the hall of the ICU to the bank of elevators; he stops jamming his thumb on the down button.

"It's her call."

"Well, I'm vetoing it."

"You can't."

"Charlie needs her. I need her," I half-yell, realizing it after heads turn our way.

"I need her, too," he whispers with a sheen of tears in his eyes.

We drive to the small diner on the corner in silence, but there's so much to talk about.

My cell vibrates in my purse. It's Gabe. But I don't want to talk to him in front of Dad.

"Go ahead answer it. It's him, isn't it? Your lover boy."

Wishing the leather seat would swallow me whole, I nod my head.

"Sometimes I wish you were still the little girl I bounced on my knee and ate crayons," he sighs shoving a hand through his hair. He parks getting out. "You want the usual?"

I nod.

"Call him back. I'll be inside."

My father is cool as hell, despite how embarrassing the last few hours have been.

"Fanny?"

"Hey." I grin despite everything, "I saw your press conference."

"Welcome to my world. It's insane."

"Yeah, I get that. But why? Don't misunderstand me—I know you are a star athlete, but so what? There's dozens of you scattered at different universities."

He's quiet.

"I wanted us to get to know each other more.... Dammit. Fuck, I'm sorry, there's just no time for that now. My father's a federal judge. He was appointed by the President. There's pictures of me hanging in The White House. My family is connected, babe. Actually, scratch that—my father's connected and I want nothing to do with him."

I suck in my breath, "So this is never going away, is it? Whatever you do will be scrutinized and reported on."

"Pretty much. Can you—will you—still be with me?"

"I don't know. When we met, you were just this cute stranger that said the craziest things."

"Cute?"

"Okay, fine, Hot-crazy-handsome-stranger, with a terrible singing voice."

"Now I know you're lying."

"Be with me, Callie. Stick with me through this. You make me feel like I can do anything."

"I don't know. My mom—she needs a bone marrow transplant. My baby brother's a match, but she won't allow him to do it."

"What can I do?"

"Nothing. She's being stubborn."

"I need to go. The NCAA and the athletic director want to see me. Can I see you tonight?"

"I don't think so. I can't go home. There's cameras everywhere."

"Fucking hell. I'll take care of it, baby."

By the way, his voice sounds—I believe him. He's sounds ready to go to war for me. I like it. *A lot.*

"Callie..." My father begins, and I'm not sure who feels more awkward.

"This boy, Gabe. I hope you know what you are getting into."

"I don't. I don't know at all. But I like him a lot."

He sighs, looking down at his plate. "Well, I can't say I'm thrilled at seeing my daughter all over TV and the Internet."

My face heats, tears prick the back of my eyes. "I'm utterly mortified."

"I don't see how you can go back to the café or the marina now. It's a zoo. He might be your boyfriend, but I'm your damned father. I'm not putting you through that, despite how badly we need to keep the businesses open. I'm shutting the café down."

"No. You can't. I can handle this. Please, Dad. I—I won't let you down. Mom needs you and Charlie. I can already tell that having you here has raised her will to fight. We need to stay open. I've seen the books... summer is when we make enough money to live."

"You are more important than money, baby girl."

"I'm not closing. I'm not quitting, and I'm not running away to hide from the consequences of anything I've done."

He sits back, sips his coffee regarding me in silence. Finally, he nods. "Okay then. I know now without a doubt, I raised you right. You're quite the woman I always hoped you'd be someday and I'm damn proud. But please do me a favor—go slow with this boy, I can't handle any more surprises in the morning papers."

"Okay. But he's hardly a boy. He's a grown man."

"Don't remind me." He sighs sitting back, throwing down his napkin.

NINETEEN

GABE

HER HOUSE IS DARK. Dressed like felon, I hide in the shadows. The hood of my dark gray sweatshirt is pulled low over my face. Her phone goes straight to voicemail.

I'm not the only prowler milling about. The damn paparazzi never gives up. But neither do I.

Slinking back into the shadows, my feet light, I tip-toe as much as a giant like me can in between the rows of beach houses dialing Banger.

"Gabe? Man, you are taking some heat, eh?"

"Fuck. You have no idea. Callie's gone. I can't find her anywhere. Her house is vacant. I need some intel. Do you know where I can find Sophie?"

"I do. But don't tell her you got her address from me. I might've walked her home from Comber's the other night."

"Jesus. Don't fuck with my girl's best friend."

"I'm not. I kind of dig her."

"Christ, *you better*."

"Hang on; I'll text you her address. And Gabe—if you ever

want to come back on the morning show to tell your side of things, I'm here."

"Thanks, bro. I just might take you up on that."

He sends me the text, and I jog a few blocks over to Sophie's. It's after midnight, but a few lights are on inside. I don't know why I don't just knock on the front door. Instead, I walk around back, grab a few small stones and pepper the upper corner window that Banger said was Soph's. I texted him back curious as to how he knew that—he said it'd be a story for later.

The lights flick on in Sophie's room; two faces stare back at me. My hand flings my hood off just in case they mistake me for a prowler or worse—paparazzi.

TWENTY

CALLIE

"Thanks for letting me crash. I kind of freaked out when I saw the press trucks lining my street.

"It'd freak me out too. By the way, remember Sara from high school?"

"Yes, of course. We had English Lit together."

"She's lifeguarding this summer—said they have a few boats off the beach with camera's pointing at your house. They haven't figured out which one Gabe's staying in yet. Word is they are hitting up the realtor's looking for rental agreements."

"Well, they won't find it since he's not renting. His coach is letting him stay at a family cottage."

"What are you going to do Call?"

Shrugging my shoulders, my hand fluffs the borrowed pillow she gave me, "I don't know. I'm just going to have to get through it. My family needs me to keep the shops open. Besides, I've already paid my summer tuition. I can't leave. There's nowhere to run."

"Do you hear that?"

A few taps coming from... the back window?

"Yeah, I do."

Flinging off the sheet, I get up from her trundle bed the same time she springs from her mattress.

"It's Romeo."

"What?"

She opens the window, the two of us gaping at Gabe standing like a warrior in under the moonlight. It shines across the sculpted planes of his handsome face. His amber eyes burning as he looks up at me.

"I can't... can't breathe without you."

My knees give. Soph just about faints as she whispers, "Go. Go, Callie. Life's too short; you know that. If you don't—I might twist my own bedsheet into a rope and climb down to him myself."

"I heard that. I think Banger might have a problem with that."

She flushes in the dark. "*What?* What did he tell you?"

"Nope. I'm not saying a damn word until you send my princess down to me."

Soph practically shoves me out the window. "Fine... I'm going—but out the back door." In minutes I meet him out on the beach.

"Hey."

"Hey." I smile back. He takes my hand, darting in the shadows. "We can't take the beach, right?"

"Or the road."

"Well, if anyone calls the police on us for sneaking through their property... we're good."

"Your uncle, right?"

"Yeah. He set up a barricade around my house, but it didn't work. They're all camped out by the curb."

"I'm so sorry. I just wanted it to be you and me. Boy meets girl... they have an epic summer—"

"... and the rest is history?" I add.

"Well, yeah."

"It's okay. Getting to know you is worth it."

He stops by the corner of hedges between two property lines. "Let's try this again. I don't see any cameras. And if there are—we'll just break the Internet again."

He pushes the hair back off my face, cups my jaw and pins my body up against a stucco wall. His kiss is relentless; thorough—as if he's tasting me for the first time all over again.

We pull apart as loud yaps come from inside the house. "Busted again." He smiles taking my hand again just as the sliding glass door opens ten feet from us.

"Run!" I yell as a chihuahua tears ass after us. He's nipping and yapping, as an old lady peers into the dark after him wondering what in the hell he's chasing. Us—a two-hundred-fifty-pound almost pro athlete and me, the shy girl from down the beach whose naked pics with said man went international.

"The poor thing is stopped at the canine fence." I giggle looking over my shoulder at the small dog's face so pissed that we were making out in his yard and he can't do a damn thing but watch us make a clean get away.

"Wait..." I ask breathless, not from exertion but at how high he makes me feel. For a moment there in the shadows—I forgot everything, even how sick my mother is. "Where are we going where no one will find us?"

"My coach's cottage. No one knows I'm there."

"Are you sure?"

His eyes find mine, hot with promise of things to come. "Yes. I swear to you—no one is going to fuck with you. If they do—I'll kick the shit out of them." We slip past one more house reaching the cottage.

He keys in, flipping on a table lamp.

I'm suddenly nervous not sure what he's expecting tonight. There's no doubt I want to be with him, but I'm once bitten, twice shy when it comes to sex.

He senses me hesitating. "Come in Callie. I won't bite unless you want me to?"

Ignoring the smirk, and sexy eyes testing me I walk over to his fridge. "I'm starving... *for food*. I haven't had much of an appetite all day."

His face turns red as he falters. I've never seen Gabe less than one-hundred percent cocky confidence.

"I lost my summer job."

"What as the rental cop?"

He nods, "I was causing more traffic than I was stopping. I'm slim on groceries and cash. Will you still want me if I can't even afford to feed you?"

"Ugh. It's bullshit how much money the University makes on athletes and yet you all are poor and starving until you go pro."

"Some don't even get that far. How did you know all that?"

"My uncle called earlier... he gave me an earful. You've got a fan in him. I wish I could've seen the look on his face when I finally confessed you were the one I stole the campus cruiser from. He wants to meet you. He already invited us over for a cookout this week. So, that will solve at least one meal..." I pause, pulling out a jar of peanut butter and handing him a spoon to share.

"I'll feed you, baby," I pat his face. "I own the café in town remember?"

"I can't freeload like that."

"You won't be. You'll have to pay me back in kisses."

"That I can do." The metal spoon clatters in the sink as he drops it to lift me in his arms carrying me to bed.

"Don't worry. My head knows it's too soon, but my heart's telling me this is right."

"Oh yeah?" I look up above him as he lays me down on his bed. "And what's your body telling you?"

"That I need to make you mine."

"Gabe?"

"Yeah?"

"I've only been with one person," I bite my lip looking down at his chest, "And it was only once. I-I want to, but I'm nervous."

"It's okay," he answers softly leaning on one elbow. "I'd be lying if I didn't tell you I want you—badly. But I want a relationship with you more."

"Who are you? Guys don't say things like this."

"They do. But only to the girls, they want to be with. I just need to hold you tonight."

"We can do a little more than that." Sitting up halfway, I yank Soph's borrowed shirt over my head and toss it to the floor.

His eyes widen at my breasts in a satin ivory bra.

"Can this go too?" His finger traces the seam around the smooth fabric.

"Yes."

He grins sliding down my body to kiss my tan skin, taste me everywhere while making me burn to be touched in dangerous places. Places that will get us in trouble despite what we just said.

In his arms, I forget the world. There's only pleasure. Burning desire, breathy moans, and roaming hands.

Each touch, each taste in the dark more decadent than the last. It's like nothing I've ever felt before. I'm not Callie—I'm just a hot-blooded woman in the arms of a demi-god whose feasting on my body like I'm ambrosia.

"Gabe," I breath sliding my hands down his back. "I want you. I'm on fire for you."

He lifts his mouth from where he was sucking at my neck. Through the underwear, we left on I feel him pulse against me.

"You sure baby?"

"Yes. Please...I need this."

"I can make you come without going all the way."

"I know. But it's time I left my past mistakes behind me and make new ones."

"Oh?" He smiles against my breast, "the only mistake we might make is doing this too much."

His hand slips between my legs rubbing through the slickness, prepping me for him. His finger draws circles lazily around my clit then slides in deep, both of us moaning at how good it feels.

"I can't wait to be in here," he moans against my throat.

"Then come on in. I'm waiting."

"I'm going to come in my pants again. You're so fucking hot."

He slides his briefs down; my eyes follow his huge cock springing free. The thick head swollen and glistening with precum. He grabs a condom from the bedside drawer and places it on the bed.

"Do you trust me?" He asks taking himself in his hand and gliding up and down his monstrous cock from root to tip.

"Yes."

"I want to feel you come, bare."

I nod, biting my lip having no idea what in the hell he's saying. All I can think about is having him inside me, finally making me feel what sex should be about.

He slides between my thighs, nudging my knees farther apart as he guides the tip of his dick between my slit. "Oh...." I moan feeling the thick tip slide in. His hips thrust forward, arms grabbing the bed rail as he goes in so far and deep, caressing places where never endings rejoice because they've never been touched.

He stays in deep, jerking back a few inches and rocking in my body. One hand coming down off the rail to touch me.

My head thrashes back and forth. I've heard about a woman's G-spot but thought it was a myth.

"Come on my cock Callie. I'm trying to last but damn you feel so good."

His fingers press more insistently against my clit, rubbing the tiny spot furiously while the tip of his dick hammers my G-spot.

The sound of the headboard slamming mixes with my shouts of "Oh God," as I come on his cock like a good girl.

He stays as long as he can; feeling me ride the wave. I feel him twitching hard and hot deep inside me, and in this moment of insanity, I don't even care. I want him to lose all control; the way he's made me. But he pulls out instead, my eyes watching him come on my belly. Spurt after spurt lands. His eyes close and open, he bites his own lip, hands rubbing his shaft as he comes looking like a sexy Chippendales model all tan abs, chiseled cheeks and fucking bedroom eyes full of passion as they land on me.

"Fuck that was good," he breathes when it's over.

He collapses on top of me, not caring his stickiness is everywhere.

When I nod, he chuckles kissing my bare shoulder. "That was just a prelude to what I can do. Imagine when I put the rubber on and really fuck you."

When our hearts stop beating like a race horse's he scoops me up taking me into the bathroom.

"In." He orders with a playful smack to my butt.

"Where are you going?" I ask as the spray hits my skin.

"Condoms."

"Oh, god," I moan, hands braced against the tiled wall. He wasn't kidding. Guess athletes have stamina on and off the field. I only hope I can keep up with him.

TWENTY-ONE

CALLIE

Warm lips fall on my forehead. "Callie? Babe? I'm heading out."

"Huh?" I rollover sleepily feeling a million dots of pleasure shoot through my body. Aftershocks from everyplace this gorgeous man touched. With my hands pressing against the tiled shower he took me from behind, his long length reaching deep inside. I never knew sex could feel so good. His fingers stroked me as he hit my G-spot over and over again while he whispered in my ear how much he wanted me—how good I felt on his cock and when he came. I felt the gushing load fill the condom when he was deep inside me.

"I'm leaving for my workout."

"Mmm... okay," I reply in incoherent grumbles still lost in the dream, I was having about him.

"Go back to sleep, princess. I just wanted you to know in case you woke up and I wasn't here." I'm wiped after the emotionally draining day I had yesterday and my new lover pleasuring me until practically dawn in ways I've only read about Christian doing to his Anna. But Gabe is only fifty shades of mine and I'm not letting him go. He thinks he's caught me, but truthfully, I'm the one in disbelief he's mine.

We talked in sleepy voices after our libidos were sated. He told me about his parents' bitter divorce, how his father cheated. And how seeing his mother's utter devastation made him vow never to be a cheater. In any capacity.

That's why the scandal rocking UVA is hitting him harder than one could ever know. It goes against his core principles, to the oath a teen boy made to himself about the type of man he wanted to be one day. The kind of man—who's caught my heart and is heading straight to the end zone.

I confided in him about how my mom's refusing to do the one surgery that could save her. How foolish I felt for giving my heart and body to Elliot one summer. My dreams of being a doctor and how I might have to put them on hold to run the family businesses.

Gabe opened up about his regrets at not entering the draft last spring. He said if he knew what was brewing he would have, because now being a top pick or even playing his senior year seems to be hanging in the balance. He said he wanted to make his mom proud; though she's not here to see it. They were very close. She died unexpectedly of a heart attack a few years ago and the pain of it still lingers for him every day. I feel so much closer to him because he truly understands what I'm going through with my mother's illness.

Sighing, I get up to pee, checking my phone.

Sophie texted that she and her mom are going to open the Blue Hydrangea saying the media is already camped outside waiting for it to open.

I text back thanks and that I owe her big time. She sends a smiley with a bunch of kissing lip emoji's.

Climbing back into bed, I hug his pillow, smelling his scent in the bedding, wishing he were still here. Since I don't have to be at the café, I have the perfect idea of how I can help Gabe.

Sighing, I reluctantly put his pillow down to get dressed. I scribble a note for him and head out into the early morning with my heart feeling light again.

He's brought back my smile and the hope that I can still be happy despite everything life is throwing my way.

"Callie?"

"Hey, Gina. I need a favor..." I feel the silly grin lighting up my face, but I can't stop it.

"Oh?"

"I need a bike...for the rest of the summer."

"I already gave you another one. Don't tell me that one got crushed too? Or stolen?"

"It's not for me. It's for him."

"Yeah... I saw that my niece is quasi-famous now."

"He needs my help."

"Sure he does," she snorts.

"He does. He lost his job. His father's a big jerk and Gabe has his pride but no food. I thought if we gave him a bike to ride he could save money, not needing to gas up his SUV. He could also use it to train. I was also hoping, maybe you could give him a few shifts here?"

"Ah, Callie. You are America's sweetheart. Sure, besides if he's here business will boom, and I can keep an eye on him."

She leads me out front where she unlocks a deep red sports bike. "It's the best one I have, good for off-roading as well. Just tell him not to wreck it."

"I will."

"Here." She hands me a helmet, water bottle and some gear, stuffing it in a new backpack she lifts off a rack. I try to take out my credit card, but she shakes her head. "Consider it a donation to a starving athlete."

"Thanks, Gina."

I adjust the seat throwing the pack over one shoulder. It's awkward, but I manage to pedal the huge bike the half mile back to his cottage. Leaving the bike and gear by the front door, I let myself in, finding him in the kitchen chugging a bottle of water.

"Babe? Where did you go?"

"Come with me." I grab his hand leading him to the front of the house. "My family also owns the bike shop in town. This is yours for the summer. I thought... you could use it instead of your gas guzzling car, and maybe it'll help you train...," I trail off feeling stupid.

"It's perfect. You're perfect. Thank you," he whispers cupping my face kissing me tenderly.

His stomach growls causing us to break apart. "I'm hungry too. We can sneak in the back door to the café and have Mike make us something special."

"Oh yeah? Am I your charity case now?"

"How about, just mine?"

"Definitely." He answers picking me up and carrying me back to bed.

"I thought you were hungry?"

"I am. I'm starving," he replies lifting up my shirt, yanking my bra to the side and rolling a nipple with his tongue. My hands clutch the back of his head to my breast. He was right— the two of us together are a live wire, burning hot. I never want to leave this bedroom, even if a tidal wave was about to hit. I'd want my last moments to be locked in his embrace while the two of us move as one.

"Play hooky today? Then we can bike to campus together later. I'll work out while you're in class?"

"You are so bad... turning me into a total slacker."

"You are the hardest working woman I know. When's the last time you took a day off?"

"Like never."

"Do it."

Sighing, I text Wes asking if he has everything under control at the docks.

He texts back that it's been slow. So far, no reporters have found me there since the business is in an LLC with a generic name as the holder. This time my tummy growls causing us to laugh.

After we shower together, we walk down the beach hand in hand. He has a ball cap pulled low over his head and a dark pair of sunglasses on. He even put a cap on my head and had me braid my hair.

I lead him off the beach a few streets from the café, sneaking around the building, darting behind the dumpsters and knocking on the back door.

"Callie?"

"I'm starving. Feed us."

"Get in here," Mike pulls my hand, looking left and right, then shuts the door quickly behind Gabe bolting it.

"They were here all morning, hoping one or both of you would show. The press is more determined than the seagulls waiting to steal the trash from the bins."

I lead Gabe over to the small table in the corner by the window. "This is where I used to sit with my crayons and coloring books when Mom and Dad worked their shifts. As I got older, I would get off the bus and do my homework right here. I loved the smells of the kitchen while I worked."

Gabe smiles, "You had a good childhood?"

"The best."

"I did too. I never did tell you, why I'm such a great singer."

"Oh, do tell. I need to hear this story."

He leans forward hunching over the small table with the red and white checkered cloth covering it. "My mother was in her early twenties in the eighties... she worked for MTV as a solid gold dancer."

"My dad would've love her. He had a thing for Sheena Easton."

"No shit! Anyway, we would watch her dance on old VHS tapes and sing along. She was so much fun. My father was always working trying to make a name for himself, so it was often just the two of us. She loved Broadway shows, too. I can't even tell you how many times I saw CATS."

"Sounds like she was an amazing mom and friend."

"She was the best. I miss her every day." He looks down, but not before I saw the searing pain in his eyes.

"Hey." My hand covers his across the table. "You are an amazing man. I'm sure she had a lot to do with that. You're so incredible I can hardly believe it."

"Told you—I was good." He winks.

"Stop." I playfully smack his hand.

"Thank you," he whispers picking up my hand, kissing it. My heart melts at the look in his eyes as he gazes at me like I'm just as incredible as I think he is. Gina was right—falling is magic when it's with someone like Gabe.

"Okay, you two lovebirds. Here you go." Mike places two steaming plates in front of us. Gabe got served breakfast and lunch. The steam from his scrambles eggs making my mouth water.

"I figured, you probably eat a lot."

"I do. Callie, please let me pay."

"Nope." I wave my fork with a home fry stabbed on the

prongs at him, "I got you a job at the bike shop if you want it. A few shifts here and there... it's perfect too because the hours you'll work will be after close just washing them down, putting air in the tires and tidying up the shop. Gina hates working nights. So, it should work out."

"You are my lucky star. I knew it. I'll make this up to you someday babe when I have money and can treat you good."

"Stop. You treat me like a queen as it is. I don't need anything, just you."

He sighs, closing his eyes, "Maybe, getting accused of cheating on my exam was the best thing that could've happened to me because it led me here—to you."

Mike rolls his eyes as he flips burgers at the grill. "I didn't sweat my ass off cooking food for you—only for it to go cold while the two of you make moon eyes at each other."

"Mooneyes?" I mouth, giggling.

Gabe winks, "Yes, sir."

We knock knees under the table, hold hands, eating with our other ones. It's the best lunch date I've had. The summer breeze blows through the open windows, Mike sings along with the radio, and the smell of burgers on the grill fills my nose, as the man who makes my heart beat faster threads his fingers through mine like he'll never let go.

TWENTY-TWO

GABE

IF ANY PAPS ARE OUT all they'll get are pics of me shirtless feet pounding the sand as I race to the close out my fourth mile.

I can't believe I dipped into her bare yesterday. But I couldn't stop myself. That girl makes me crazy; wild with lust that shuts down any common sense. But it's not just her body I crave. What first drew me in was her sassy mind, quirky sense of humor and her fire. I was a goner that night she stole the car and laughed as she drove away.

But I know I'm clean. Hell, I've had enough blood drawn to fill a blood bank. Every test coming back negative. I've never had sex without a condom. Except the one time, I woke to Jackie riding me, taking advantage of my morning wood.

I threw her off quickly, wrapping up, but I was unsure how long she was on me.

I lost my head yesterday and despite Callie telling me she has herself protected—I won't be the man who screws up her dreams. Especially since mine are getting so royally fucked with. We had the best time together last night. After class, we stayed at my place, curled up on the sofa watching old movies and eating popcorn. We talked as much as we kissed, eventually making it to the bedroom.

Stopping in the wet sand, I get down on my elbows, rising into a plank. Waves hit my back, rinsing off the coat of sweat clinging there, cooling me off. I hold it for three minutes then change positions and bang out two hundred push-ups.

Getting back up, I sprint for three minutes then jog when I round the part of the beach where Callie lives. I took her key with me hoping to get her some things. The houses dotting this section abut to the public beach, where Gran's cottage has private beach rights. Sure, as shit—twenty men with fingers hovering above fancy Nikon cameras attached to tripods wait. All of them pointed at the back of my girl's house.

I can get in... but how in the hell am I going to slip out? Looking straight ahead, my fingers reach inside the zippered pocket of my shorts finding the key. Sprinting past them, the sounds of rapid clicks are followed by shouts. But I'm fast as fuck and no match for men who stand around all day.

Safely inside, my fingers twist the bolt. I help myself to a bottle of water and walk upstairs to her room.

Instead of feeling like an intruder, I feel like her home is already my home as I stare at photographs of her and her friends scattered around her room. But one picture stops me cold. It's of her and what must be her mom. They have matching chocolate hair and smiles that would brighten any room.

I wish there was something I could do—something I could give, to make this right for Callie.

Putting the picture back on her dresser. I open her closet and find a duffel bag. I've never had a sister but have been in enough relationships to feel comfortable packing her bag.

Twenty minutes later, it's all zipped up and ready to go. Jogging back down the stairs, I pause by the front window, raising a few blinds with my fingers.

I'm trapped.

They know I'm inside.

Sighing, I take out my phone and google the Sea Spray PD. Hitting call, I grin as it connects to dispatch.

"911 what's your emergency?"

"Hi... this is Gabe Parker. I'm trapped inside my girlfriend's house. You might know her? Callie Anderson?"

"The chief's niece?"

"The very one."

"Well, hang on son. I'll send the swat car."

"That really won't be necessary."

"Honey... we've been dying to test it out. It's been sitting here since March."

"How is that going to help me get home unnoticed?"

"We're the police. We're pros. Do you need me to stay on the line with you?"

"No, I'll be okay," I chuckle.

She hangs up. Then it occurs to me—the pictures of me getting into a SWAT car are going to go viral. Shit's going to hit the fan again depending on what the captions say under the photographs. But maybe it'll give them something else to go into a frenzy over—something other than pictures of my girl captured beneath the moonlight.

"Holy shit," I mutter ducking my head, using Callie's duffel to shield my face as four armed officers meet me on her stoop, escorting me into a kick-ass Humveed-up van. Five minutes later and after signing autographs they drop me off at the bungalow. Anxious to see my girl, I jog into the house, stopping short.

"Banger?" Sweaty and tired as hell my fists clench at him sitting at the table while Callie serves him breakfast wearing my shirt and no bra. At least not that I can tell.

"What happened to you?"

Dropping her bag, I grab the TV remote hitting the on button fro the local Sea Spray channel.

"Gabe? Why are you being escorted out of my house by SWAT police."

"It was the only way out, babe."

"My father's going to hit the roof if his head doesn't go right through it."

"Damn, bro. You really know how to make an exit. You're a born celebrity. If football doesn't work out—Hollywood will be knocking at the door."

"Not interested. I hate the press."

"Maybe, so. But they love you."

"Whatever." I shuffle over to my girl, grabbing her around the waist as she fries bacon.

"Ummm," my fingers snatch a few from the hot pan before she can whack them with the spatula in her hand. "Where did this food come from?"

"Banger. He ran out to the corner market when he found me opening all these empty cupboards."

She won't look me in the eye; her cheeks wear a natural blush as she feels me staring down.

"Ah, my shy little princess," I murmur against her ear, "your bad wolf is going to ravage you as soon as I get rid of him." Giving her a playful smack on the ass, I chug the glass of orange juice she poured for me eyes glaring at Banger over the rim, telling him to stop looking at her ass.

He smirks, raising a brow challenging me.

So, I hit him where it hurts.

"Babe. Did you and Banger hit it off? Did he tell you how he hooked up with Soph?"

"What?" She spins so fast; I have to catch her. She stalks towards him all bed hair and wild eyes.

"It's not like that. She's sweet. We just kissed, I swear." He holds his palms up to halt her advance.

"Don't mess with her, Banger. Soph isn't some summer slut."

"No, she isn't."

"You like her, don't you?" My girl asks.

"Maybe." He's evasive; I need to jump in and rescue him. Banger's been here for me. He's a new friend, but his loyalty is that of a best one.

"What' up anyway?"

"I have news."

I take a seat across the table, grabbing Callie's arm as she serves me a hot breakfast. Taking her hand, I place a kiss on the inside of her wrist. "You don't have to serve me, babe."

"I know. But I wanted to."

Banger rolls his eyes, finishes chewing his food then continues. "My father's representing you."

"What?"

"Yeah. He's a big-time lawyer in Georgia, that's where I'm from. The only thing he loves more than winning a case is football."

"I-I can't pay him."

"It's pro-bono, man. Every hour he helps you is a tax write off."

"Are you sure."

"Absol-fuckin-lutely."

"Shit," I let out a breath with a hiss. "Thanks. I needed a break."

"Trust me. My dad representing you is going to be a total game changer."

My eyes find Callie's as she sips her coffee, "I hope you're right."

Banger stayed for another half hour before I kicked him out and took my girl back to bed where I made love to her gentle and slow. Hips and lips saying what I can't with words—not yet. I gaze into her beautiful eyes as we come together, perfectly as one. My hands lock hers above her head as my dick pulses deep, hitting her spot. "Babe, God, Callie," my eyes shut as my dick jerks, blowing my load in her again. I feel her inner walls clenching me with her own release.

"I could love you someday. Someday soon," I whisper against her hair, hands coming down to cradle her face as I kiss her sweetly, still emptying myself into the condom.

Her dark eyes don't answer. They're full of pain.

"Babe?"

"Don't leave me," she whispers. "Everyone I love leaves me."

"Never. Never," I swear, kissing her again.

She sighs beneath me, hands clutching the back of my head. My heart sputters and stalls. I'm a goner. My heart's sunk to the bottom of her ocean locked up tight in her tiny hands.

"Stay in bed with me? I don't want you having to deal with idiots today."

"No. I have to go in. I'm not a coward. Besides, you need to get your second work out in at the gym. You're getting soft." She giggles squeezing my bicep.

My dick stirs against her thigh. "Nothing on me is soft, baby."

Slipping another condom on, I roll her to her side going in deep, realizing she basically admitted she loved me. I held he ran my arms never wanting to let go, but I know she needs to get to work. After we shower and dress, I drive her in. She's cute as hell in tiny khaki shorts, tennis shoes and a teal polo top. Her long hair is pulled back in a high ponytail.

Before she can swing the door open, my arm blocks the handle, "Where's my kiss?"

"There are cameras everywhere."

"So? They've gotten worse shots."

"Don't remind me."

But she tilts her head to mine, kissing me sweetly. I growl low in my throat not wanting sweet. Every time I see the press —I see red, wanting to stake my claim that this girl is mine and if they fuck with her I'll kill them. My hand moves to her head, our lips fuse as my tongue takes hers over and over. We're having sex with our mouths.

Click. Click-click-click.

My car is surrounded, but I don't give a fuck. Let them take all the pictures they want. There's nothing wrong with a man kissing the girl he loves.

Holy fuck. I'm in love.

Although I've been in long-term relationships, I wouldn't say I've ever really been in love. Until now. Until Callie.

She breaks away needing to breathe. "How am I going to get out?"

"Just open the door hard and push them out of the way. Don't let them loiter. At least make them buy something."

"Our sales are up sixty-percent since the story broke that we're dating."

"See? I am good for something, besides my huge—"

"Shut-up!" She slaps a hand over my mouth giggling, "They probably have professional lip-readers on payroll."

"Who cares?"

"Ummm, I do? Hello? My parents still watch the news."

"Ancients."

"Har-har. Don't forget we're going to my Uncle Steve's house tonight for a cookout."

"The Chief of police?"

"Yes."

"Great."

"Don't worry He's a huge fan."

"Those are the worst. They talk my ears off all night about plays and how I can improve my game."

"I think your game is just fine."

"I thought you said you don't watch football."

"I don't. But you still scored me."

"I did, sweetheart, I did." I cup her face for another quick kiss before she takes a deep breath, opens the door hard and runs through the crowd.

I don't know what possesses me to say it.

Watching her struggle and fight them off, kicking one in the shins makes me grin. As she runs towards the door, the words just gush out.

"I'm falling in love with you!" I yell through the open passenger door.

She freezes, hand on the door to the café. She turns around. The crowd is going wild! Cameras point at me and her bouncing like a tennis ball at Wimbledon back and forth over the net.

"I'm falling in love you with you, too!" She yells back with a grin, "Even though you're a horrible singer."

"Oh yeah?"

"Yeah!" She puts a hand on her hip daring me.

This is so us.

Public displays of PDA or dares.

Putting my SUV back in park, I roll down all the windows open the sunroof, and scroll through my phone connected to the Bluetooth speakers.

She's never going to guess this one. Finding the soundtrack to Dirty Dancing (the original) *I blast I've had the time of my life,* stand up, my thick forearms go through the sunroof first, my head and shoulders following. Her mouth hangs open as at the top of my lungs I start belting it out.

People start dancing.

A few woman pretend to swoon. Hell, maybe they actually do.

It's a street party at ten a.m.

But the best part is when I reach the part where Jennifer Grey runs into Swayze's arms. My girl runs to me, uses her foot to vault up the open passenger door, stands in the frame her hands gripping the roof as we kiss.

"Now that's a love story!" Someone whistles as clapping erupts around us.

"You are such a goof."

"You love it," I answer.

"I do."

"By the way...you left your laptop up. When I went to get it this morning...I couldn't help but see all the royal wedding stuff on your Pinterest board."

"Snoop."

"Yup. But I'm your prince charming baby."

"Are you going to give me the fairy tale?"

"Planning on it."

We kiss on the top of my car, with the crowd around us. It's almost like being on top of a carriage, right?

"I need to go. See you later, goofball."

"Later babe."

With the stupidest grin on my face, I watch her walk to the café. This time the crowd parts, everyone lets my princess pass.

An hour later the first ping hits my phone.

I made myself a Google alert, so I'll know when anything with my name hits the Internet. There it is. My new headlines:

"From Dirty Player to Singing Prince. How Gabe Parker wooed his lady love."

"If the NFL doesn't work out; sign GABE PARKER up for American Idol. That boy has some pipes!"

"GABE PARKER is a showstopper on and off the field. Who knew UVA's Star wide receiver has a voice of solid gold?"

Getting a screenshot of the headlines, I text them all to Callie.

Me: See? I am good.

Callie: It's a sing-off tonight. My Uncle Steve has a karaoke machine. He' s good.

Me: I can't wait. Are you challenging me?

Callie: Yes.

Me: It's on. Winner takes all.

Callie: All of what?

Me: All of each other.

Callie: if there were an eye-rolling emoji I'd be sending it right now.

Laughing, I slip my phone in my gym bag, ready to lift hard today. She makes me feel so damn good. Now, I just need the rest of my life to straighten out.

TWENTY-THREE

CALLIE

"Are you nervous?"

"No, why? Should I be?"

"Babe. You're bringing this stud home to meet your family."

"Not all of them—only the cool ones. Besides, Gina already loves you."

"What can I say? The Anderson women find me irresistible."

"We do." I stand on my tippy toes tugging him down for a quick kiss. We had to drive to Steve's place. He lives on the bay side of Sea Spray nestled behind a nature preserve on two acres of marshes and inlets. It is peaceful out here with nothing but crickets, swaying sea grass, and music already floating from the back patio.

We walk in hand in hand with matching goofy grins. Uncle Steve sizes Gabe up in two seconds. He must've passed the test since he hands him a beer and a playlist. "No thanks. I'll take a water, though."

"Training hard?"

"Something like that."

"Not hard enough, if our little C, over here can give you the slip and steal your ride."

"You heard about that, huh."

"Laughed my ass off for days."

"I did, too. She has spunk... I have to admit it's partly why I fell for her."

"Partly?"

Gabe grins, staring back at Steve hard. Some secret man-to-man communication passes between them. Finally, Uncle Steve nods his head, "Come on. I made Portobello mushroom sirloin burgers with Swiss cheese. Food first then we sing."

"I might have to marry into this family."

"I'm available!" Gina laughs, hooking her arm through Gabe's, introducing him to the crowd of cousins and friends on the way to the food table.

"Gabe Parker, huh? You caught a really big fish, Callie."

"Oh, I didn't catch him. He caught me."

Steve throws back his head hooting out, "She's a live one, Parker. You better hold on."

"Oh, I intend to," he replies from across the patio. The way he looks at me is still the same. Even though we've become lovers—he still looks at me the way he did on the beach by Comber's—possessively, hungrily, like I'm the world he wants to conquer.

It's enthralling, being wanted by a man so virile and smart as him. But he's so much more than just a smart jock. He's funny, charismatic, caring, a total dork at times, but I love him. Love him for being all those things combined simply into a man who looks at me miraculously seeing things—I don't even see in myself.

TWENTY-FOUR

JACKIE

CRASH! MY HANDS PICK UP whatever objects are near throwing them left and right.

Two years.

For two years—I starved myself, only eating lettuce and drinking water. I can't remember the last time I had real carbs.

All that. And he never told me he loved me.

I can't believe he said it to that... that... that—cow!

I can't stop myself from looking at the video on YOUTUBE again. Gabe's through his sunroof singing to her. "FUCK!" I scream, throwing my hairbrush so hard it cracks the mirror. Shards of broken glass fall all over my vanity, coating my Mac makeup brushes.

The video of him proclaiming his love to that washed up piece of seaweed already has over one million views.

He's blowing up Instagram and twitter too.

It should've been me. I should've been his princess.

Instead, I wasted two years sweating my toned ass off in hot yoga classes, enduring hunger pains, racking up credit card debt—dressing myself like a WAG for a pro player, and it was all for *nothing*.

I practiced my smile making sure it seemed sweet. I even lied—told Gabe I was a virgin, purposely making sure I was just ending my period the first time we had sex so that he would believe it.

Maybe that's why we lasted two years. I know Gabe had a hard time dumping a girl he thought saved herself for him. Gabe always was too noble for his own good. I thought I'd be able to hang onto him long enough to get his ring on my finger and his brat in my belly. Not that I ever really wanted kids. But his kids would be moneymakers for life. I'd hire nanny's—he'd be on the road traveling so what would he know about it? I already had a plan to claim post-partum depression and get out of even holding the thing.

Slamming the lid of my laptop down, I walk to the window of the apartment I rent just off campus.

That cow isn't stealing my happy ending.

She's not riding off in the new Maserati I'm sure he'll buy with his first pro paycheck, no. Uh-uh. If I can't have Gabe's genetically superior babies, she's not either.

I just need to find their castle and crumble it to the ground.

Picking up my cell, I call the PI the law firm I'm interning at uses for their divorce cases. He's slimy, always giving me the creeps. But as long as I flirt with him and pretend I don't notice him smacking his lips as his eyes check out my MasterCard paid C-cups...he gives me information. For free. I just need a little bit more before he starts wanting to charge me on my back or knees. Hell, I might even do it—if it means ruining Gabe forever.

"Jackie?"

"Did you find where he's living in Sea Spray?"

"Yeah, but it'll cost you."

"I figured it would."

My head spins as I lower the phone, contemplating a way to make Gabe and that girl pay. Stepping around my trashed room, I throw some clothes in a weekend bag. It looks like I'll be spending a few days by the shore.

TWENTY-FIVE

CALLIE

JUNE TURNED TO JULY in frenzied minutes of waiting tables and slow seconds spent in Gabe's arms as he took me to the stars. The amount of media frenzy slowly died down, but a few stragglers remain, hoping to get another money shot of Gabe. I've practically moved in with him. Well, okay, I have moved in with him. I've spent every night for the past month in his bed and woken up every morning to him making love to me hard and slow.

I'll never get enough.

He's turned me into a nymphomaniac.

Sometimes he comes to the marina, pulling me into a supply locker, turning me around and taking me hard and fast.

I like it both ways.

I'm proud to say the town folk have my back. My family goes back generations here, and they've circled the wagons around us. My uncle loves Gabe. They hit it off like I knew they would. They even text and call one another—daily. I'm almost jealous. But it warms my heart that two of the men I love most in the world are becoming friends.

Our life is almost perfect.

We drive to campus together. When I'm in class, he lifts weights, and when he's in class, I study in the library.

At night we cook together, laugh together, study and make out under the stars.

Somehow, we went from a first date to a couple living together as if we're married.

Despite, how insanely happy we are, we both have black clouds offshore ready to storm at any second.

Gabe's waiting a final hearing with the Board and NCAA to see if he's clear to start pre-season next month. Banger's father, Rick Higgins is no joke. He had them sweating under their collars when he countersued everyone. The school—the NCAA—Jackie and a few newspapers that published complete crap. Gabe's image is turning around, especially since his musical debut outside the café last month.

He even drove with me up to UVA to volunteer for field day at Charlie's camp. He was so good with all the kids. They loved him. I took him to meet my mom and dad when we were there.

Mom embraced him like a long-lost son. Dad was not as easily won over. But I guess that's to be expected when he was the only man in my life for twenty years.

I'm hoping Gabe will know soon if he's able to play. UVA is shitting themselves, bending over backwards to explain why Gabe was even suspected of cheating in the first place—especially when Jackie caved and admitted she never actually saw Gabe take any illegal drugs... and he passed every academic and drug test they threw at him.

Jackie cried in front of the camera claiming all the attention made her have a miscarriage. Gabe admitted, he thinks he was only with her for so long because he was still reeling from losing his mom.

But Rick's not letting it go. He's demanding a court-ordered release of her medical records to prove she's a liar. It will help Gabe's case if they can prove she lied about it all—and her credibility as a witness in the University's probe will be destroyed.

My feet dangle over the side of the dock. Most of the slips are empty. Every Fourth of July we typically sell out. It's peaceful in mid-morning. It's just me the birds and the sound of the tide slapping against the rocks.

"Callie."

I don't turn around feeling awkward around him.

"How are you?"

"Fine," I reply without even glancing in his direction.

He sits down next to me despite my best attempts to be unfriendly.

"I'm here if you need to talk."

"Talk about what?"

"Look—I know I screwed up. We were both young—I was being pulled in so many different directions. Anyway," he sighs rubbing the back of his neck, "I know what it's like. My family is always in the press."

"I know. I've seen you over the years."

He looks at me, wanting to say something but holds back. "It's true then? You're with Gabe Parker?"

"She is."

We both turn our heads as Gabe stands on the upper pier behind us. He's not happy. The sculpted lines of his face are furrowed, eyes narrowed as he gazes down on Elliott sitting close to me.

I stand, jogging up the steps to him, put my arms around him and lay my head on his shoulder. I feel his lips graze the top of my head as Elliott mutters from below. "I guess you are." He hops on board the Sheena Easton and unties the lines. Seconds later the boat leaves the channel for open water.

"What's his story?"

"That's Elliot. He—we, kind of dated a few years back."

"Oh? Is he the one—"

"Yes," I answer cutting him off. I don't want to go there. Never again. I just want the man who sings me to sleep every night and wakes me with his hands and mouth.

"How was the exam?"

"Aced it as usual."

"Of course, you did," I grin as we walk inside. The first summer session is over. Gabe and I both have a break for the Fourth of July. We're meeting Dad half-way between here and UVA because the traffic is insane. He's dropping off Charlie for the week, and I'm so excited. I've missed him so much and can't wait to take him mini-golfing and to the beach.

"I'm going to miss sleeping next to you." I confide holding him close as the office door bangs shut behind us.

"What are you talking about, babe? I'm coming to your place for sleepovers. I'm not leaving my woman and her baby brother alone in a house all night."

"We'll be fine."

"Maybe. But I won't. I can't sleep without you now."

My insides turn to mush. "Fine. But he can't even catch you coming in and out of my room. And no sex with him in the house—sometimes he has night terrors."

"Night terrors?"

"Yeah, it's awful. It's a bad dream that he can't wake up from. The doctor says waking him only makes it worse."

"Poor guy. We're going to make this visit extra fun."

"We?"

"Yup. You're stuck with me, babe. I always wanted a little brother. Besides, I make kick-ass sandcastles."

"I'm sure you do." I wrap my arm around his waist as we walk up the dock to his car.

TWENTY-SIX

CALLIE

HUGGING MY KNEES TO MY CHEST, my eyes turned towards the horizon, I can't imagine a more perfect day. Gabe packed a picnic lunch, drove Charlie and me south to a state beach park where no one bothered us.

We had a blast playing in the waves with my little brother.

"Cawwlie?"

"What's up buddy?"

"Is Mama gonna die?"

His question takes me by surprise since he seemed happy all day. But I guess we all carry our scars deep where no one can see them.

"No."

"You promise?"

Gabe meets my eyes over the top of Charlie's sandy brown head, "Yes. Of course, she is." I turn my head away before he sees the tears of uncertainty welling in my eyes.

"Are we ready to go? Pirates Cove is calling..."

"Yes!" And for the time being—his question is dropped. But I know it won't be long until it's answered.

"He's quiet. He must be asleep."

Gabe turns his head quickly, his eyes softening as he glances at Charlie in his booster seat. "He is."

"We should just go home then. We'll save mini golf for tomorrow morning before we bring him back."

"Want to order in?"

I link our hands together where his rests on my thigh. "I'm tired, too. That sounds great."

He lifts my hand to his lips for a kiss and I settle back in the seat, drifting off as he drives us home.

"Callie."

His voice rouses me from a deep sleep—the kind so deep you don't dream but wake confused and disorientated.

My eyes blink open. It's dusk. I'm in his car... in my driveway. Something's not right... but I can't process what it is. Gabe's looking at me like my world is about to fall apart. The anguish in his eyes makes every hair on my body stand on end.

Then looking past, him, my eyes fall on my Dad's truck parked by the curb.

My body processes faster than my sluggish brain. Hands frantically unfastening the seatbelt trying to get inside.

"Wait." His strong hands brace my shoulders. "Charlie's inside. Don't... your Mom doesn't want him upset."

"Let me go."

His hands fall as he steps back. Sprinting across the small lawn, I fly up the steps, throwing the door open. She's in my spot. Sitting on the sea wall watching the waves like we've done a million times.

Charlie's asleep in the hammock and my dad... he's sitting with a beer in his hand looking as lost as I feel.

This can't be happening.

It's like I'm watching the ending to a movie when you wished the director filmed an alternate one. One in which everyone gets their happy ending.

But I'm not sure if that's meant to be this time.

I feel Gabe standing at my back, his arm comes out to hold me, but I step forward brushing him away.

On heavy feet and with a heavier heart, I move forward against the tide. I don't say a word as I sit next to her on the wall, staring straight ahead.

"I used to believe if I stared hard enough—I could see the future in the waves." She turns placing her pale hand on mine. The ends of the scarf she wears around her head rustles in the wind.

"It's time. I'm going home. I needed it to be here. Where I can feel the sun on my face and the wind on my back."

"No. No!" I sob, "Do something!" I scream at my father. "Make her get the surgery."

"It's not his fault. It's no one's fault," she whispers.

"I'm not accepting this. How... how can you leave us? Without a fight?"

"I'm tired. I've been fighting, Callie. But I don't think I'm winning this round."

"I-I can't accept that. Please, keep trying!" A knife cuts through the center of my chest, tearing my heart and soul apart. The keening sound coming from me unrecognizable as belonging to any human.

"Babe."

Gabe tries to pull me back against his chest, but I jump off the wall, racing towards the water—wishing I could keep running for her as much as me, that fate won't catch up with us.

"Callie!" He shouts, but my mother's soft voice follows, muffled by the breeze. She must have told him to give me space.

My legs keep running past the burning stitches in each side

of my abdomen. My lungs burn, too. But I keep going chased by things I can't outrun.

Finally, I collapse down on the sand where it clings to my sweaty skin. I'm not sure how long, I stare at the waves trying to read the future.

"Hey."

Ignoring him, my eyes never waver from the ocean.

"Callie?"

"Go away."

He ignores me, sitting down in the sand.

"What's wrong?"

My chin quivers. I break like the surf I'm staring so hard at. "My mom's dying. She came home to die, and I have to watch it happen."

"At least you get to say goodbye. Sometimes you don't get a chance."

Through helpless sobs and streaky tears, I stare at him. "Like you never said goodbye to me? How could you? I-I thought the summer we spent meant something to you... then you just up and left after everything we shared? It took me years to get over you!"

"I-I know. It took me years to get over you, too."

"Really? I find that hard to believe, especially when I saw your face all over Instagram and Social pages."

"You should know now, more than anyone what that's like. What they print and what the truth is don't always match up."

"Yeah, I guess so. But what how you left me—was really shitty, Elliott."

"I'm sorry."

"Thanks, but it's years too late and I don't need to hear those words from you anymore."

"Well, I still mean them."

Standing up, I'm blinded by flashes. "Get out of here!" Elliott roars, standing in front of me.

Sand and mascara fill my eyes, I swipe both away trying to see. Through all the faces, shouts, and flashing cameras; a pair of eyes stand out from the rest. There's something about her that's dark—evil as she smiles smugly at the camera's capturing the utter destruction on my face.

A shudder runs through me, but I can't break her stare. She mouths, "Game over." Her perfectly bowed slick lips smiling.

My gasping sob seems to enrage Elliott even more. He charges, grabbing cameras smashing them together, throwing some behind us in the water. He's wrestled to the ground but fights his way up throwing punches left and right.

Sirens wail in the distance coming closer. Looking around, I realize I ran straight into a summer cookout at the wealthier section of the beach where Elliott's family usually stays. I don't see them, but plenty of people my age.

Officers pant as they race down the beach trying to break up the ensuing fight.

"Cuff him! He destroyed my property!"

"The hell I did. You're on a private beach!" Elliott roars the veins in his neck popping.

"Callie?"

"Hey, Vin. He's with me." I point to Elliott.

The photographers are pissed as Elliott is freed and they are forced to leave. But I'm sure enough of them got pictures of me.

"Come on. I'll walk you back."

He's breathing hard, still pumped full of adrenalin as he walks beside me. "Thank you."

He shrugs. "I'm sorry. They came out of nowhere."

"I ruined your party." My eyes flit to the overturned kegs and tables. Food is scattered in the sand.

"Eh, I'll have more."

He picks up a shell; it's perfectly white with no chips. "For good luck."

"Thanks."

I take it, accepting it for the peace offering it is.

"I can make it from here."

"You sure?"

"Yeah." He tries to hug me, but I shrink bag. His hands fall to his sides.

"Right. Take care, Callie."

Giving him a sad smile, I turn away, knowing he watches me walk all the way down the beach until I reach home.

The house is just as dark and silent as it's been for weeks.

"Hello?"

"Gabe took them out for ice cream."

He's sitting in the shadows in the same place I saw him last.

"Are you drunk?"

"No, but I wish I was, Callie girl."

"Ah, Dad. I-I just can't believe this."

"Neither can I. But it's what she wants."

"What about what we want?"

He shrugs.

"I'm going inside."

Plodding up the stairs to my room, I strip then get into the shower. I'm able to rinse all the grit, tears and sand off my skin, but I don't feel much better.

I can't eat.

I can't sleep.

I'm stuck—in limbo, with nothing to do but wait. The melancholy that takes over my heart wins. When Gabe calls, I hit ignore. When my cells pings with dozens of texts—they go unanswered. My body and mind are both full of dread. I'm tired of the press—of being chased. Tired of being strong all the time—shouldering so many burdens. When sleep finally takes me away from it all, my mind is full of memories of my mother teaching me how to ride the waves.

TWENTY-SEVEN

GABE

I FEEL SICK.

Staring back at me is my girl's beautifully haunted face. It's destroyed. Her soul's cut-up for the world to see. And they are.

The photographer captured the essence of the moment so well I'm sure he'll win an award.

But what's fucking me up more than that is *him*.

He's the one there—kicking the shit out of them—doing what should've been my job.

Someone at that pricks party recognized Callie and tipped the paps off. I want to rip his head off—tear him a new one while I'm at it just because he had what's now mine.

I don't even want him breathing on the same planet as her.

"FUCK!"

Her phone goes straight to voicemail. I wanted to stay last night, but she wouldn't let me.

I kissed the top of her head telling her I'd be back this morning but she never once mentioned that any of what I'm looking at even happened.

The only reason Elliott isn't in the slammer is because of Steve—I'm sure of it.

I text him, and he texts back, confirming my suspicions. Elliott trashed thousands of dollars' worth of cameras and equipment and would have faced assault and battery charges for breaking a few noses. But when Steve found out he was defending Callie, he made sure the charges went the other way —sticking the paps with trespassing and parking illegally.

But the real thorn in my side are the headlines.

"Gabe Parker's new love falls back in the arms of her old flame."

"Has the Player been Played? Gabe Parker's girl-friend caught canoodling with her ex."

The sky is gray filling with storm clouds, fitting my mood. My cell rings on the counter, but it's not her.

"Coach?"

"Parker. I was calling just to make sure you're not trashing Gran's house or doing something stupid to jeopardize the team. I just got official word—you're cleared. The University and the NCAA has nothing. Not one shred of evidence that you ever cheated in class or on the field. Congrats, son. Your banishment is lifted. I expect you back in two weeks for pre-season."

"That's great."

"Well fuck, Parker. Can you sound any happier about it? I busted my ass all summer for you son, making sure this shit didn't cling to you."

"I—I appreciate that. I do. It's just shit's hitting the fan here. My girl—her mom's dying. The press is crawling over the sand like fleas—I need more time. Here with her."

"I thought you got it. I thought you understood? If you want to play at the next level—you need to keep your head clear. No drama, no women, no bullshit juvenile heartache screwing up your career."

"She's important to me."

"More important than football?"

"Maybe."

"I expect you back in my field house by three p.m. on August 8th. If your ass isn't sitting in my locker room getting padded up—consider yourself cut. You can kiss your scholarship and any chance of going pro, goodbye. Choose wisely."

I set my phone down, needing to think.

I love her.

There's no doubt I do. But should I sacrifice years of everything I've done to achieve my dream? Is it even wise to give it all up for love?

We need more time together. She'll be with me at main campus in the fall. But how can I leave her here—all alone with a terminally ill mother, a broken-hearted brother and a father so caught in his own despair he can't move off his chair?

I can't.

But I didn't fight so hard, for so long to go out like this either. Picking up my phone, I scroll finding Steve's number.

"Yo! What's up, Parker?"

"I need a favor. A big one."

"Shit. Does it involve the SWAT van again?"

"No. I wish. Listen—I need you to kidnap someone for me."

"No. Uh-uh. I'm not getting involved in your love affair with my niece."

"Not Callie. I need some time with her mother, Gayle."

"Christ, Parker. Seriously?"

"Just do it. Callie can't know. No one can—that we're meeting. Just set it up. I'll get you season tickets, behind the bench."

"Shit. Fuck me... alright, I'll do it. I'll need some time—for logistics."

"Figure it out. I need to be back on campus in two weeks."

"Fuck. Fine, I'll text you."

Grabbing my keys, my thoughts racing, I drive down to the marina.

"Gabe?"

My long legs jog down to the dock where Wes is pumping diesel into a small fishing boat.

"I need a favor. Maybe a few."

"Parker?"

Turning, my eyes meet Eric's, Callie's father. "You finally moved."

"I couldn't just sit, watching the light die in her eyes."

"She's that bad?" Wes asks.

"I'm not talking about Gayle."

"Callie?"

"The cancer might be taking my wife's body, but it's also killing my little girl's soul."

"You have any boats unrented? Ones we could sleep on for a few days?"

"Sure, but do you have a license?"

"No. Callie does, right?"

Without missing a beat Wes drops the fuel hose, motioning me to follow. "This is her favorite. It's forty feet of pure fiberglass and teak wood. Sails like a dream, too."

"What's her name?" I whistle taking in the sleek sailboat that hasn't been here all summer.

"Saving Grace. The couple who rented it sailed up the coast of New England for two months. They just got back yesterday."

"You can't go out today. There's twenty to thirty-foot swells being reported."

"No. Not today. I was thinking more like tomorrow?"

"Fuck." Her father whispers under his breath.

"Look, Eric. I know why you hate me. I get it. Wherever I go, camera's follow. I can't promise that it will even change now that I've officially been cleared to play. My dream's always been to go pro. I'm not going to stop until I catch the winning pass in a Super Bowl. But I love your daughter, more than my next breath. All I'm asking is for some time with her. Away from everything—while we still can."

"Fine. But you'll need to be the one to convince her to go. She won't leave her mother's side."

"I know. But I'm praying to God she won't leave mine either."

Patting Wes on the back, I give Eric a curt nod and jog back up to my car. I have a lot of preparation to do, to get this right. I just hope she comes.

TWENTY-EIGHT

CALLIE

I DIDN'T SLEEP THROUGH THE NIGHT. I kept thinking it's not real. My beautiful, once vivacious mother can't be dying in her forties.

But she is.

And there's nothing I can do about it.

The home phone rings and I answer it before it wakes Charlie.

"Hello?"

"Callie? It's Dr. Klein—your mother's oncologist from UVA..."

"Yes. I know who you are."

"Your mother...she left quite unexpectedly... against my wishes. I have her latest scan results... may I speak with her?"

"Sure—hold on."

"Mom?" Tapping lightly on her door, I peek in. But the bed's empty. Through the window, I see her slowly walking on the beach.

Racing down the stairs, I jog barefoot across the sand to give her the phone.

"It's Dr. Klein."

"No." She shakes her head.

"Mom?" I hold it out, determined she takes it.

She shakes her head, turning back down the beach.

"She won't speak to you. Can you give me the results?"

"I'm afraid I can't. It's against HIPPA guidelines."

"Can you speak to my dad?"

"Yes. He's on the list of people she cleared to talk about her health record."

"Okay. Can I have your office number?"

"How about I give you my cell, instead?"

Jotting it down on a piece of paper I found in the kitchen, I tuck it into the back pocket of my jean shorts.

He's jogging towards me, but there's no light in my heart today. It's gone black. Sitting on the sea wall, with my legs dangling, I wait.

"Hey."

"Hey."

"Why haven't you answered my calls?"

"I'm sorry. I—it's just been a lot."

"I know."

"Come with me?" He holds out a hand.

"Where?"

"Away... just for a few nights."

"I can't."

"Yes, you can. I need you, too. Besides, I've already cleared it with Eric."

"Eric?"

"Yah. Your dad and I are like this..." He takes his hands pressing them together.

"Yeah, right." But he does get me to smile.

He leads me into my own house, upstairs to my room, packing my bags like he did only a little over a month ago? It seems like I've known him forever.

"Where are you taking me this time?"

"Actually, it's where you are taking me. Out to sea, on Saving Grace."

"What? She's back?"

"She is and all ready for us to go." He slaps me on the ass, playfully.

"Oh, but according to the press—we're over. Didn't you hear I dumped you for my ex?"

"Never." He drops my bag hauling me close for a kiss. "We'll never be over."

But the pit in my gut tells me nothing lasts forever. I know that more than anyone.

"Cawwwlie?"

"Hey, Charlie, what's up?"

"You promised to take me boogie boarding."

"I know, bud. But there was a storm offshore yesterday that caused a riptide."

"But we can still make sand castles, right?"

"Sure. How about it, Gabe? Are you up for it? We can sail off later tonight."

"Absolutely."

Jumping off the wall, I gather Charlie up in a big hug. "I love you, buddy. You're my number one man."

"Hey!" Gabe laughs hugging me from behind.

"Sorry. You're number two."

"I guess, I can live with that." He replies, hugging me from behind.

"Can you pack up some snacks?"

"Sure."

While Gabe gathers the snacks, I pack up our beach gear then write a quick note leaving it on the counter that we'll be down the beach. During low-tide a small tidal pool forms that's full of shells, crabs, and critters. Charlie loves catching and releasing them when the tide rolls back in.

"Ready to go?"

Two heads nod. "Okay, let's do this!" I smile for Charlie's sake, but I'm struggling hard, pretending to be fine.

It's still only mid-morning, but the beach is starting to fill. We trudged a half mile down to the tidal pools and set up.

Gabe has a fisherman's hat and Ray Ban's on. But there's no disguising his huge physique as he takes his shirt off and sits in the sand next to me.

"Do you want to talk about it?"

My throat closes. "No. Not here. Not yet."

"I understand. You know I'm here for you, right?"

I nod as he covers my hands with his.

"I'm sorry about yesterday."

"Me, too."

He sighs, kissing the top of my head, "Come on. Let's make Charlie the best sand castle this beach has ever seen."

The clouds break, letting the late July sun shine down hot on our backs. We take a break, sit under the umbrella, sharing snacks. The warm sun makes me sleepy, and I doze off as Gabe and Charlie chase crabs.

———

Shouts jolt me awake. Confused, I sit up finding myself at the edge of a crowd. Annoyed, I stand, bolt forward and push my way through. A few try to elbow me aside until I'm recognized. I'm angry that another peaceful day has been ruined. I just want to grab Charlie and go. But when I finally break through the mob of photographers and reporters—it's just Gabe trying to shield my mother from the fray.

"Where's Charlie?"

Their eyes frantically search. "He was just here... "

"Charlie!" I turn screaming. "CHARLIE!"

Gabe raises his hand above his eyes, scanning the beach in all directions!

My mother frantically looks in all directions, unsure which way to go.

"We need to split up. I'll search the water," I swallow hard. "Gabe you head towards home..."

"I'll alert the lifeguards," my mother cries in anguish trying to run in her weakened state. Gabe takes off—he's there in two minutes shouting frantically. Mom falls in the sand under the weight of anguish. In seconds she's surrounded by flashing cameras.

While our hearts are in our throats—they don't help. All they do is click and click, documenting the panic; the fear. My anger boils over.

"HELP! HELP US!" I scream. "My five-year-old brother is gone! And it's all your fault!" In disgust, I shove a few to the ground, running for the water. I sprint into the surf, diving straight under the crest of a breaking wave. "CHARLIE!" Frantically, I dive under opening my eyes fighting the sting of salt as I search underneath the water.

I don't even remember if we put his swim vest on since we were playing in the tidal pool.

Wave after wave slaps my face as tears fall and I scream his name.

"Callie!" Gabe grabs my arm, but I shove him away diving under again.

He hauls me up out of the water. "They found him."

"Where!"

"He's okay. He's by the concession stand."

Sprinting out of the surf with Gabe right beside me, I don't care about the cast of onlookers gaping. I just need to get to Charlie and make sure he's safe.

"Charlie?" He's sitting with an ice cream cone in hand flanked by two lifeguards and a bike cop.

"Cawwlie? Am I in trouble?"

"What happened buddy? You know not to run away." Kneeling down in front of him, I cup his face.

"I didn't. I wanted to help."

"Help who?"

"The pretty lady who lost her puppy."

Holding him close against my chest, his ice cream smushes against me but I don't care in the least.

"What did she look like, bud?" Gabe asks, placing a hand on his head.

"Pretty. Very pretty. She was crying, scared that her puppy got scared by all the cameras. He can't swim. So, I helped her look. But then she remembered her friend took him home, so she bought me an ice cream for 'my troubles.' When I looked up, she was gone."

"Did she tell you her name?"

"No."

"What color hair did she have?"

"Blonde like Rapunzel. She had pretty eyes too. Very blue. She had a nice smile and smelled good—strangers, aren't pretty and smell good, right?"

"Sometimes, the evilest people are the prettiest ones on the outside, bud."

"She said. You were bad." He points at Gabe.

Gabe kneels down next to me. "I need to ask you one more thing," he hangs his head, taking a deep breath. Taking out his phone, he taps the screen then holds a picture out for Charlie to look at. "Was this her?"

"YES! See? I knew she wasn't a stranger."

"Who is that?" The police officer asks.

"My, ex, Jackie Delaware."

"I'll call it in."

Gabe calls Steve at the same time cop presses the radio clipped to his shirt and speaks into it.

"Steve? Yeah, we have him. It was my ex, who took him with some bullshit story about a lost puppy. Yeah, ok, will do."

"Take him home. I'll get your Mom and our things."

I can't even look him in the eye. I love him, but everywhere he goes—chaos follows.

TWENTY-NINE

GABE

IT'S BEEN THE DAY FROM HELL. I've never been so scared as I was in the ten plus minutes Charlie went missing. It happened so fast. One minute, I was shielding Gayle and him from the paparazzi—then in the next, he was gone.

Fucking Jackie.

I knew she had problems but attempting kidnapping? That's only one of the charges she's facing. The Sea Spray police found her flashy Mercedes stuck in traffic. She obviously didn't plan her getaway very well. She attempted to lie her way out of it claiming that she indeed did have a puppy. But no one bought it. It turns out she was holed up in a cheap rental. Steve called telling me to meet him there.

Closing my eyes, I rub my fingers over my lids sitting back in the driver's seat. I drove out to the bluffs just needing a minute.

Jackie is borderline certifiable.

She had pictures of Callie and me everywhere. Well, what was left of Callie after she cut her haphazardly out of the photos. She left scribbled notes with dates and times of where I was. Obviously, she was the one tipping off the media. Now that she's behind bars, I'm hoping shit will calm down.

But somehow, I don't think it will.

Callie's home number flashes across my cell.

"Babe?"

There's silence. "It's Eric. She doesn't want to see you. I called Wes and canceled your romantic getaway."

"Hate me much?"

"Can you blame me? Ever since you came into our lives—my daughter's been dragged through the press both clothed and unclothed; my son got kidnapped and my wife dying from cancer is your latest victim. Images of her kneeling broken in the sand made the front page.

"Fuck."

"Exactly. Take a page from the playbook—take a knee and let the clock run out."

"I can't do that. No offense, sir, but I'm a born fighter. I'll never stop fighting for your daughter."

"Sometimes... you don't always win. It's just the way it is."

He hangs up.

"FUCK!" My fists punch the wheel. Tearing the driver's side door open so hard I almost take it off the damn hinges, I storm out of the car. With my hands fisted in my shorts, the wind blows hard as I stare at the pounding surf slamming against the rocks below.

The clock is running down. But I'm not taking a knee. I don't have much time, but I'll be damned if this is the way everything ends.

Hunching over, I sit on the ledge, thoughts as wild as the waves crashing beneath me. In my heart, I know there was some truth to Eric's words. I was victim to things out of my control—the cheating allegations, suspicions of doping, the press capturing sacred moments with my girl and now Jackie's twisted plan of revenge. Steve thinks she planned to do worse and actually take Charlie somewhere. In her rental, we found maps of state parks with hiking trails highlighted, zip ties and rope. But at the last minute, she just left him there with an ice cream cone.

Thank fuck for small miracles.

But I'm resolute in what I need to do now. I've felt it for days—this overwhelming need to give Callie the only thing left —hope.

"She still doesn't want to see you." Sophie stands in the door cracked open by three inches.

"I'm not leaving."

"Suit yourself." The door shuts in my face.

There's no more story to get besides the one sure to print in tomorrow morning's edition.

Shuffling around back to the side of the house, I take a seat on the sea wall right on Callie's favorite spot.

"I always wanted to make the front page. But not like that." Gayle's voice comes from the shadows behind me.

"She won't leave Charlie's side. Even sang him to sleep. She blames herself more than you—she won't forgive herself for falling asleep."

"She's exhausted. Worked her ass off this summer between the café, marina, and classes."

"She won't have to do that anymore."

"Because you're giving up?" I mutter, springing up, angry at her; at the world, for not giving Callie and me a clear path.

"How dare you speak to her like that?"

"Callie?" I breathe, my heart stopping in my chest as she walks out of the shadows.

"I couldn't sleep. I came out to clear my head... needing to think about us. Thank you for making what I'm about to say easier."

"Don't. Don't baby." I rush forward placing my index finger against her lips.

She steps back.

"It's too much. I can't, Gabe. Please understand..." She breaks off, tears glistening in her eyes.

"I do understand. But it's all behind us now. I've been cleared of everything... Jackie's been detained... she was the one tipping off the press about everything."

"But there will always be the next Jackie. Someone—somewhere, trying to tear us down."

"I wish I could stand here and promise you there won't be. But it's part of being a professional athlete. But don't you trust me—believe in me—that there will never be anyone else for me but, you?"

She shakes her head. "I can't. I can't give my all to making a relationship with you work when I need to stay here, spend these last months with my mother. Then eventually, I'll finish my degree. Who knows where you will be? How would we ever make it work when your season starts next month and after that —your professional career? You could end up anywhere. Besides, I'm not sure I'm cut out for the life you're destined to live."

"The only place I wanted to end up—was with you. But I can't keep chasing you, Callie. I won't. At some point, you need to meet me—halfway."

"I know. I'm sorry."

"I love you," I step forward, hands cupping her face as I kiss her one last time.

She nods, trying not to cry.

THIRTY

CALLIE

Love.

It's so precious, makes you both strong and weak, but when it goes—it's cruel—ripping you apart into a million shreds. He hesitates wanting to say more but stops short. He looks at me for so long his gaze is a magnet drawing me to him, but I've flipped over, and this time don't move. I stand still, melting from the heat in his gaze as it roams over me one last time before finally turning away. My breath comes out in a whoosh. I was so consumed in him I forgot my mother was still here until she speaks. "Forget cancer. The look he was giving you—even gave me heart palpitations."

"Was that a breakup? I'm not even sure."

"I think it is... unless you change your mind. Go, Callie. Run after him—change your mind."

"I will—if you will."

"Brat."

"Well, you raised me—so if I am, it's on you."

"I'm in the mood for a hot fudge sundae with extra

whipped cream. Now that chemo's ended, I finally want to eat. Are you in?"

"Sure. But only if that includes finishing season two of The Crown."

"Ah Callie, girl, I have a feeling this family hasn't seen the last of Gabe Parker."

"How can we? When he's everywhere. Now the ghost of him will be everywhere, too. I'm sorry, I don't feel like ice-cream anymore." Choking back a sob, I run to my room, my chest is so tight I can't breathe.

Elliott.

Gabe.

Mom.

Somehow circumstances always leave me with the remains of love that's left behind.

THIRTY-ONE

JACKIE

"I'M INNOCENT. PLEASE... BELIEVE ME." I bat my mink eyelashes at the officer, pouting demurely. But he's not buying it. I should have kept up with my acting classes.

"His name was Bailey. He was a rescue pup I picked up by the side of the road. Please, he's out there..." I break off. He stops, standing closer. I hide my smile, noting that my cleavage is popping since the cuffs are still on pinning my arms behind my back. He leads me to the interrogation room. It'll be my fifth time today in that room.

"Do you even understand the trouble that you're in?"

"No? I didn't do anything..."

"They have you on surveillance."

Dammit. I didn't think of that.

"Can I at least use the bathroom? I've had to pee for hours."

He grunts stopping outside the restroom releasing me from the cuffs.

Ugh, I look like roadkill. No wonder my superior damsel in distress routine isn't working. Wetting a towel, I wipe the smudged makeup off, biting my lips for color. My fingers work through the tangles in my hair, and I fluff it a few times.

Not bad.

"Times up." He raps on the door.

I walk out hoping my primping does the trick. "Turn around, hands on the wall."

"Yes, officer." My voice was breathy, and I made sure to stick my ass out as if I'm getting ready to be plowed from behind. Gabe always made me come so hard that way.

Gabe.

It's all his fault. He had to go get the perfect sweetheart of a girlfriend, live in that perfectly cute beach house, getting ready for another perfect season.

But I'm far from feeling perfect. But I'll be damned if he's going to win. I'll find a way to come back out on top.

I'm fucking Jackie Delaware, beauty pageant winner at Oklahoma's state fair three years running, former pageant queen and the future Mrs. Somebody.

The cuffs bind my wrists again, but I'll admit it's kind of hot. Maybe that's where I went wrong. I should've been freakier in bed.

Yes! That's it! I'll up my bedroom game, get into that kinky BDSM shit that's all the rage and make myself into the perfect little beauty pageant slut with just enough class—my next mark will go insane if he doesn't make me his little "*wifie.*"

"Ms. Delaware?" A fat, balding man stands up, spectacles perched on his nose as I enter the small room. "I'm Carl Rogers, Sea Spray's public defender. If you confess maybe the judge will show leniency since you have no record. You might get away with community service time."

"I didn't do anything. He was lost, I bought him an ice cream."

"That's not what the boy is saying."

"He's what? Five? His mother's sick....it's my impeccable word against his."

"They have you on tape."

"At the concession stand, buying ice cream like I said. I found him nearby; I did something nice.

"They found your pictures and notes in your rental."

"Well, shoot." I bat my eyelashes, "So, I didn't handle my break up well. Since when is a broken heart a crime?" I bend over the table, noticing how his eyes shift to my girls. His hand comes up to loosen the tie around his neck. I bet that's not the only item of clothing feeling tight.

"So, what do you think? Are you good enough to get me off?"

His face turns red at my double entendre.

"I-I'll try." He stammers like a fool.

"Try hard. I have somewhere I need to be." My mind's racing. I'm done at UVA, but there are plenty of other colleges in the south filled with athletes who could go pro. I need to get back to campus and fire up Google. Whoever I find with the most potential... that's where I'll put in for my transfer. I could start fresh—hell, I could even change my name to Jackie Parker after all. Wouldn't that just be fitting?

Laughing so hard I can't stop; my attorney looks at me as if he's scared out of his mind. "We could say your break up caused you to suffer a mental breakdown...."

I laugh harder, like Cruella de Vil. I belong in a Disney film, but I'm not the princess—I'm Ursula, the sea witch with better hair. And one of these days—the evil queen will reign.

THIRTY-TWO

GABE

THE POUNDING OUTSIDE MY DOOR has me springing up from the couch. She came.

I knew she would.

Hitting pause on the game tapes Coach sent by Fed-Ex, I hurdle the couch to get the door.

"Parker! Where's the party? We're all safe and have one week left till Coach hands us our asses in pre-season." Marcus, Trey and Logan, our new QB from Tampa, crowd the front door.

"The three of you smell like desperation. Did you douse yourselves in an entire bottle of Chrome?"

"Hey—the pickings have been slim on campus this summer. We're on the prowl for beach honeys tonight. Besides, we heard what Jackie did. I always knew that bitch was no good."

"Yeah, bro. Get dressed, we need to represent and what you got on won't do it." Marcus eyes me, before heading towards the fridge.

I shrug not caring in the least that I'm wearing flip-flops, gym shorts, and a white undershirt.

"Damn, homes, there's no beer? What are you onto now, the hard stuff?"

"I didn't drink all summer. I was training hard."

"Yeah, that's not all you were doing..."

"Shut the fuck up, Trey," Marcus warns as my fists clench.

"I'm sorry man. She was just a summer hook-up, though, right?"

"No. She wasn't." I open the front door wide, "now get the fuck out. Before I haul your asses out."

"Whoa. Chill... we're staying, bro. I've never seen you like this." Marcus sits on the couch, crossing his legs as he props them on the coffee table.

My head drops, staring at the floor, hand still holding the door open. "I'm not in the mood for company."

"We know. That's why we're staying."

"Fuckers," I bite out under my breath.

"Yup. But we got your back, bro. On and off the field. We're going out."

"Beachcombers?"

"Yeah, that's the one."

"Fine. But you're buying. I'm dead broke."

"Done. Just remember to pay me back when you sign for first multi-million contract."

"Parker, what's up?"

"Hey, Banger." I greet him with a fist bump and a clap on the back.

"Sorry to hear about Callie's mom... and that drama with her brother being almost kidnapped."

"Yeah, last week was rough. She dumped me over it."

"Shit. That sucks."

"Yeah. I'm not getting over her anytime soon."

"Any chance you could reconcile?"

I shrug, sipping the beer Marcus bought, "it's me. The fame —it's only going to get worse. Callie needs to focus on her family and finishing her degree... somehow being with me was fucking all that up."

"My breaks about over... hang out after closing. I'm throwing an after party."

"Sounds good."

Banger takes his place behind the DJ table on the stage, lights start flashing, fog machines turn on, and the dock shakes with the force of hundreds of people jumping to the beat he spins.

I'm easily recognized after being splashed everywhere the past few months. With my practiced, forced grin in place—I pretend to enjoy the attention from the dozens of girls asking for selfies with me as they press their bare legs and arms against my side. Some even pinch my ass as they lean close, smiling.

I don't flirt or dance with one, despite the many desperate attempts to get me to.

My heart is still raw, beating only for the girl who keeps running from my love.

I'm saved from yet another girl whose had a few too many of whatever fruity cocktail she's downing, by Banger, tapping my shoulder.

I follow him through the crowd, as he leads me to the stage. "You feel like singing it out? I saw the YouTube video of you."

"Nah, my heart's not in it tonight."

He nods, placing his headphones on and leans into the mic. "All right folks, this is last call. Last call for alcohol. Good night

Sea Spray...." He plays, "Sweet Caroline." Hundreds of drunks sing into the summer night swaying with the palm trees.

"Let's get the hell out of here. There's at least three girls here that I hooked up with this summer. If I get cornered by any of them—I'm screwed."

"Jesus, Banger. I've never had a problem just sticking with one."

"I know. But the one I want—wants someone else. Unrequited love is crap."

"Yes, it is." I tip my beer bottle to his. "Fuck it. I paid Wes to stock a boat at the Marina. Even paid the daily rate for it. We can go there."

"You sure?"

"Fuck yeah, let's go."

Circling my hand in the air like a helicopter to the boys, I walk out not even caring if they follow.

"I'll drive." Logan takes my keys, and I shrug feeling pretty buzzed.

Three random girls squeeze in, sitting on laps, their high-pitched drunk giggles grating on my nerves.

Banger follows taking more people in his car.

We reach the marina. The office lights are off; everything's locked up tight for the night. But some boaters are there lounging outside having a few.

My group follows me down the dock to board the Saving Grace. Wes gave me a tour earlier, and I know where the keys are hidden. I don't turn the motor on, but I power up the string lights he hung from the mainsail to the stern lines. It's romantic as fuck and makes me want to punch something hard. Instead, I smile handing out beers and wine from the stocked cabin fridge and host an after-party when I was supposed to be out on the open sea making love to Callie under the stars.

Lost in my thoughts, I sit on a cooler, peeling the label off my beer.

"What the hell is going on?"

"A party, asshole!" I mutter at the figure standing on the dock, his face hidden by the shadows.

"Gabe Parker?"

"Yeah, who the fuck wants to know?"

He walks forward into the light.

In a split-second, my beer's forgotten as I vault over the stern onto the dock fifteen feet from him.

"Elliott."

He strolls forward, shaking his head at me, "She would've been better off with me. I wouldn't have dragged her down."

"Fuck you!" I snarl, charging forward with my fist cocked.

He bends his head charging back, arms reaching for my waist as we tumble on the docks, both jockeying for position as we land blows. He hits me in the ribs, forcing me to grunt. Chaos erupts around us as women scream and my boys try to pull us apart.

I land a few blows to that pretty boy's face, my chin snapping back as he lands one last cheap shot since Marcus has my arms pinned back.

My ribs and eye hurt like hell, both swelling, but I grin like a motherfucker as his chest heaves, eyes full of rage as we stare at one another. "She'd never go back to you. She loves me."

"Oh, yeah? We'll see about that. I'm transferring to UVA... word is your too much drama for the girl next door. I'm looking forward to getting to know her, *again*..." He trails off.

I see *red*.

With a roar sounding like a battle cry, I break free from Marcus' hold hook Elliott around the knees, and the two of us tumble into the water.

We both sputter to the surface. He's the first to break away swimming to the edge of the dock, hoisting himself out.

I tread water for a few minutes letting it clear my head. "Come on," Banger gestures, "the cops are here."

Diving under, I surface in front of his feet taking his hand.

"Gabe?"

"What's up Steve? I just felt like a swim."

"Uh-huh. Any of them underage?" He nods to the girls Marcus brought back.

"I have no clue."

"They better not be. What the hell is wrong with you? You just got your life back."

"No. You're wrong. It doesn't matter. None of it will matter —if I don't have her there with me."

"Who says she won't be? But acting like this won't win her back—being the man she fell in love with will."

"I don't know. I feel lost. How can that be when I've only known her a few months?"

"When you know, you know. I'm officially off the clock. You got any more beer?"

He claps my back, walks me back to Saving Grace and just like that my mood lifts. "You're like the older brother; I wish I always had."

At first, everyone's nervous until Steve walks back to his car to grab a change of clothes. We sit around, laughing—shooting the shit. Marcus and Trey smooch their girls for a bit, and another couple joins us from the next boat, bringing a guitar and bongo drum.

"We heard you like to sing."

"I do... and he owes me a rematch. He won our last sing-off, but it was rigged."

"Bullshit, Parker. Don't be such a baby. I was better than you."

"You were surrounded by family and your subordinates... it was a rigged vote."

"Oh, it's on like donkey-kong." Steve stands taking the guitar. Without missing a beat, I grab the drum, placing it between my legs. He starts strumming the chords to "Landslide," thinking I won't know it.

But he's wrong. I grew up listening to everything and watching Glee with my high school girlfriend every Saturday night on her DVR while we made out.

Steve is going down.

And this is just the release I need to relieve my heartache. Even if it's only for a little while.

THIRTY-THREE

CALLIE

"That didn't take long." I hold out my phone so that Soph can look at the pictures of Gabe with Banger at Beachcombers.

"Whatever. He's pulling the classic guy move—smiling with a beer in hand, with his arm around some blonde."

"Whoa. Are we talking about Gabe or Banger?"

She shrugs, walking into my bathroom. I'm glad she slept over last night. I wanted to text Gabe a dozen times and take it all back. But I can't jerk him around like that. He's leaving for pre-season soon anyway, and I've decided to put my dreams on hold again for my family. I can't leave, attending class at the main campus leaving Charlie here alone with a fading mother and a half-functional father. Charlie's going to be destroyed, and I'm not sure how things are going to go when the end comes.

"Let's grab breakfast."

"I can't eat."

"I know. But you need to."

She's right. I down the coffee already made but only end up nibbling on a bagel.

"I need to get to the marina. Dad's working the café today, so at least my feet get a break." I eye my chipped toenails.

"We need a day of beauty."

"I wish!"

She shrugs, "Why not? Half of our regulars work at the salon. I'm sure they would hook us up."

"Maybe."

"I'll ask. We should get the works at the end of summer, so we can hit the main campus looking fresh."

"I'm not going..."

"Callie? You have to. They only offer freshman and sopho-more level classes here."

"I know."

"Oh, Callie. Surely your mother wants you to go?"

"I'm sure she does. But, how can I?"

"How can you not? Is the better question?"

Shrugging, I unplug my cell from the charger, "My uncle left me a string of texts. I need to get down to the marina—he said it's urgent. Thanks, for staying over with me, Soph. I don't know what I'd do without you."

"You might not feel the same after pledge week."

"What?"

"You are going to main campus—the drive won't be as long after summer when the tourists are gone. I've signed us up—to pledge to the Gamma Omega Sorority. It's a good one; they are big into charity work."

"You didn't?"

"Too late. You've been so busy playing house with Parker to think about the fall. I've got us both covered. Even if you get back together—he's going to be consumed with football. They practice twice a day, watch game tapes at night—travel about every weekend all while maintaining their grades. And he needs to be on top of that after everything he's been through this summer."

I bite my lip, "It sounds like I did the right thing then—not saddling him with a girlfriend that would need him far too much."

"Gabe doesn't seem like a guy who would ever say that—much less think that way."

"No, he isn't. Which is why I'm doing it for him. He's sacrificed so much—worked so hard to get to where he is. I won't be the reason why he doesn't make it. Going pro was a dream he shared with his own mother. I can't even be the reason why he's off—even if it's only for one game. I need to let him go now, so he can get back to campus for pre-season and get back into his routine. By the time his first game comes—I'll just be the girl I spent one sweet summer with," I smile wistfully.

"I think you are much more than that—you know it, too. But you both have so much going on—pulling you in opposite directions. It doesn't mean you can't love him."

"I know. I've just realized how deeply I love him—I finally understand what it means to love someone so much—you can let them go."

"So, you finally understand?" We both turn our heads at my mother standing in my doorway.

"Yes." I sob, bowing my head. I wasn't talking about her, but I guess that's what she needs, too.

After quickly getting dressed, I hop on my bike, pedaling down to the marina. The clouds rolled in bringing a misting rain with them.

"What the heck?"

Gabe's car is parked right next to Uncle Steve's cruiser. Elliott's Range Rover is here too.

This can't be good.

My traitorous heart starts beating for him again. But I'm

still raw and angry over the press tearing into our lives and Charlie being put at risk. I know Gabe didn't ask for any of it, but he's a magnet drawing more than just me.

The rubber soles of my sneakers tread quietly down the dock. I pause for a second not believing what I'm seeing.

Gabe and Steve are drinking hot coffee perched on the bow of my favorite sailboat, Saving Grace. Their tan legs dangle over the side, Elliott is a few spots over, throwing the lines, taking Sheena off the dock. Gabe flips him the bird, and even from where I'm standing, I have no problem hearing Elliott mutter, "asshole," as Sheena clips by.

"Save any coffee for me?"

Gabe's head snaps up so fast he smacks the side of it on the boom. "Careful, that mast will crack your head."

"What does it matter, since this girl I met already cracked my heart?"

Shoulders sagging, I bend down taking my shoes off before boarding.

"Yep. This is my cue to leave. I don't know how you dated him anyway," Steve nods over to Gabe, "when he snores like a damn freight train."

Seeing the look of confusion on my face, he puts a hand on my shoulder, "I crashed the boat party Gabe and his buddies had here last night."

"You... you partied on my yacht?"

"Your yacht? I don't think so cupcake."

"It is."

"My parents promised never to sell her. They put the deed in my name."

"Oh yeah? Maybe I'll buy it out from under you when I make my first million." He baits me, knowing I can't help it. Just like the night we met, flames lick along my skin; burning anger and desire fuse together.

The anger helps me forget how much I want to tell him we're back on, as I peer below noticing empty beer bottles scattered everywhere.

"Why does my boat smells like piss and beer?"

"Sorry. Marcus got wasted; he might've had bad aim when going over the side."

My foot taps on the teak deck, "Where are they?"

"They left. Went to your café for breakfast with Banger, he wanted to see if Soph was working."

"She is. They better not give her a hard time."

"They won't... well Banger, might."

"What are you doing here anyway?"

He hangs his head, arms gripping the mast, biceps bulging, finally, he looks at me. "I was planning a romantic sail with you. Your father gave me the green light. We were supposed to go last night. Wes... stocked the fridge. I thought we could just go sail away, just the two of us; out on the ocean where no cameras could follow. No crazy exes, either. Yours or mine."

"Elliott's not crazy."

"Debatable."

He's hurt, looking at me like an unwanted puppy on adoption day.

"Let's go then. We need to talk anyway."

"I don't like the sound of that."

Stepping forward, my arms find his waist. He draws in a sharp breath as I lay my head on his shoulder. Tears find their way out as he holds me tight.

"This isn't over because I don't love you. It's over because I *do*."

"Don't. Don't say that. Why Callie?"

"It's too much. Your life is too much for me to handle right now. I can't keep hitting the pause button on what I want. As long as I can remember, my dream has been med school. I've given up almost everything as it is, just to keep my grades at a level where I can be competitive. I know if I kept loving you—I'd give it all up; follow you anywhere. I don't want to wake up one day—resentful. I'm not the girl content with a diamond ring, Range Rover, and a million-dollar home. I'm flip-flops, boardwalk fries, messy hair, and a ten-speed bicycle."

"I know. That's what makes you perfect."

Stepping back, I untie the lines, throwing them on the dock and start the engine. "Let's just have today. One more day, to be us—Callie and Gabe—the couple that met by accident and loved each other hard one summer."

He shakes his head, stands behind me as my hands rest on the wheel, guiding us out of the channel.

"I'm never going to give up on us."

I don't reply, trying to soak up the feel of him holding me close so I can remember it on the lonely days and nights ahead.

THIRTY-FOUR

GABE

STEVE ESCORTS HER To my car waiting at the curb.

"What is this?" She's surprised to see me.

"I'm taking you on a road trip." I grin, opening my sunroof and turning up the volume on the song I've got on. "Buckle up, Gayle. It's not always a smooth ride."

"Is that the same line you used on my daughter?"

"No. But It would've been a good one."

"Good Lord."

"I haven't even started singing yet. What's your favorite band?"

"You're too young to have heard of them."

"Try me."

"The Violent Femmes."

Grinning so hard, my dimples must be showing, I scroll through my playlist finding "Blister in the Sun." Cruising down the main drag out to the highway with the sun in front of us, the two of us sing each verse—I even slap my hands on the wheel mimicking the drums.

"It's no wonder my daughter fell hard for you."

My answer is a wink and a grin.

"Where are we going anyway?"

"Can't tell you that. Just enjoy the ride."

"The buffet at the Sagamore?"

"No. Maybe next time."

"Gabe," she warns in a low voice, "you better not be bringing me back to the hospital." Her hands start frantically trying to unclip her seatbelt.

"Nope. No hospital. Promise."

"Okay..."

"I'm hungry as fuck," I mutter pulling into McDonald's. "Oops, sorry."

"It's okay. I'm hungry as fuck, too." She giggles turns the stereo back up and bops her head to the beat. At least she's smiling for now. I'm hoping some hot fries, and a chocolate milkshake will keep it going.

"I can't believe my daughter dumped you." She sucks down her milkshake, as I alternate between stuffing my face while driving with one hand on the wheel, singing, "American Girl."

"I know. I told her I was the king of fun."

"Unlike me."

"What? Cancer's not fun?"

"Dying sucks."

"Nope. We're going to change that. Stick with me, honey."

"God help my daughter..."

"Oh, there's not a chance in hell we're over. She just doesn't realize that yet."

"I think she does. She's just too scared to admit it."

"I'm not sweating it. When my princess is ready—I'm going to swoop in and carry her off—"

"Into the sunset?"

"No. Boston. They want me... bad. From what I hear, anyway. I just need to have another epic season and stay injury free."

"I've seen you play."

"You have?"

"On TV. I'm a UVA alum, myself."

"But Callie doesn't watch?"

"No. She's hardly watches TV. My Callie is the outdoors type. If she wasn't on the beach with a book in hand, she was always out riding her bike, or down at the Marina with Eric learning everything a girl could about boat motors."

"She's so different. It's one of the things that drew me in—right from the start."

"Never stop loving her."

"I don't intend to."

"Good."

She polishes off her food, reclines her seat, closing her eyes as the beat plays.

"The football stadium? You drove me two hours to a football stadium?"

"This isn't just turf and bleachers, Gayle. Lives are made and broken on this field." Helping her out of my car, I swipe my card at the back entrance, leading her into the tunnel.

Her cell rings echoing around us. "It's Callie."

"Don't tell her that you're with me. Makeup something... anything..."

"Callie? What? No, I'm fine. You don't need to know where I am... I'm the parent, remember? What? I don't know what time I'll be home... there's no curfew for me, either. Be good. Don't throw any more wild pity parties or burn the house down baking break-up cookies. You ate two dozen at least in the past week..."

I laugh, trying to cover it as a cough as she waves at me to shut up.

She hangs up, shaking her head at me, "she'd die of embarrassment if she knew you heard about the cookies."

"It's cute as hell. Make sure she saves me some."

We reach the end of the tunnel, leading to the field and I turn to her. "I love this moment the most... the roar of the fans sound like thunder as you step to the edge, hidden from view but able to see everything. The second you take one step onto the field everything changes. You don't know which way things are going to go—but you put it all out there, leaving nothing behind."

I take her hand in mine and step forward. She stands at the precipice with me; imagining the picture I painted in her head. "I believe... that it's never too late for a comeback. No matter your age, where you are in your life—or what roadblocks stand in your way. I'm about ready to make mine, are you in?"

She takes a deep breath trying not to cry.

"It's okay—I've got you."

"I know you must think I'm terribly weak. No one understands—the pain. Not just the physical pain, but knowing this thing has a hold of your body that you can't fight. I'm tired, Gabe. So, tired of spending endless days in a hospital bed, wearing a hospital gown, smelling hospital smells. I missed the ocean, my home—my girl. I just wanted to live on my terms, even if it meant I lived for a shorter amount of time—I felt like I was taking back control. But while I did that—everyone else around me was losing theirs."

Contemplating her words, I walk forward, standing until

we reach the fifty-yard line. "Here we are, Gayle. We have three plays to get to the end zone. The first: go back for more chemo. The second: get the bone marrow transplant. The third: do nothing and let it ride. Choose wisely; you might not get another chance to play on the big field again."

She stares at me, the real deep, read your soul stare. "Thanks, I will."

She starts walking slowly, eyes on the end zone, when she turns, "walk with me?"

"Tell me about your life Gabe—outside all of this..."

"The truth?"

She nods.

"My mother was my world... then I met Callie, and I could see her being the same. I lost my mother unexpectedly a few years ago. I'll never get over it. She drove me to every practice, cheered at every game. Sometimes when I play under the lights, I find myself automatically looking for her. She used to sit at the twenty-yard line five rows deep. She said it was the lucky spot. No matter how old I was or where I played I could always find her there." I pause choking on my words as my eyes find that spot in this stadium.

Now Gayle's the one comforting me as she takes my hand. "I don't know how I'm going to leave them."

"Then don't. Keep fighting Gayle. Leave it all on the field."

"I'm afraid."

"That's okay. You get used to it."

She bends her head, deep in thought for a few minutes. "That day, when Charlie was missing... I knew I wasn't ready to go. He needs me. I can't ever imagine not being there to protect my baby."

"That's good. Keep digging...."

"Then, seeing you and Callie. I want to be there when she

gets married—even if it's not to you. I want to be there and not in spirit."

"It will be to me. Use this. Harness this to push through the wall holding you back."

We reach the twenty-yard line pausing. "She'd be so proud of you, Gabe. Any woman would be to call you their son."

I nod, suck in a shaky breath and let my tears fall freely. It hurts so damn much. Callie once told me everyone she loves leaves her—I guess it's the same for me too.

"Okay. I'll do it. You're quite convincing."

"That's good since you're not dying anytime soon. You never heard your last test results. They were better. You have a solid chance to beat it. Don't breathe a word of this to Callie. I want her to come back to me on her own. It needs to be that way. She needs to feel strong enough to enter the world I'll be living in."

"I understand. She'll get there. She's never been in the spotlight before, and the two of you were in it all summer."

"There's one more thing—Jackie had her court date yesterday. The judge gave her time served and one hundred hours of community service. I could press stalking charges... but they might not stick. Her lawyer did call mine though. She's leaving Virginia for good."

"Okay, just make sure of it Gabe. I can't protect any of my children from room one-twenty-two in the ICU ward."

"You have my word she won't step one foot back in this state."

She picks up a practice ball from the bin by the bench. "Show me. Catch!" She cocks her arm back, throwing a perfect spiral straight at my chest. I catch it running hard, feet flying over the turf as I pass the end zone spiking the ball.

"Well done."

Clapping emerges from behind us. "Lincoln's replaced. You've got some arm."

"Thanks?"

"Coach?"

"Hey, Parker. I knew you couldn't stay away."

"I'm not staying yet—I still have a few things to wrap-up but yeah Coach, I'm ready for my comeback."

"The girl?"

"This is her mother."

"Jesus Parker, that's a new headline."

The three of us laugh, toss the ball around for a bit but Gayle's fading.

"Ready to go?"

"Yes. But not home. Take me back to the hospital, Gabe. My fight starts again tonight."

"Let's go then. Should I call anyone?"

"No. Let it be a surprise. But take me to the diner first. I'm hungry as hell again. They don't feed you in there."

"Can I get you another pillow?"

"No, I'm fine."

"I feel funny just leaving you alone, like this."

"I'm not alone. Did you see the five nurses checking you out back there?"

"I did. I had to bribe them with tickets not to snap pictures."

"I'll be fine. Go, Gabe. Chase your dreams now. Don't stop until you get it, either. We made a pact tonight, remember?"

"I do. The two of us are going to make epic comebacks. I'll be back. Pre-season starts next week."

"Sneak me in another milkshake? I'm going to need it."

"Will do."

I shuffle to the door, turn down the lights, feeling optimistic. She has everything to live for, and I'm so glad she chose to fight. All summer long I wanted this for my girl. I'd give her the moon but giving her mother back is even better.

THIRTY-FIVE

CALLIE

Four months later....

THE STADIUM ROARS WITH THOUSANDS of fans
eager to see their boys play. I'm caught up in the moment with
them, standing on my tippy-toes with anxious eyes hungry for
my first glimpse of him in months.

There he is.

Number 18; helmet off, arms pumping up the crowd as he
emerges from the tunnel. Even from the distance between us, I
can't miss the gleam of hunger glowing from deep within his
eyes. I used to see that same look as I laid beneath him in bed.
But now that look is for the game.

My hands cup around my mouth as I hoot and cheer with
all the other crazy fans.

It's a crisp fall night. I'm wearing the jersey he gave me
under my North Face fleece. Truthfully, I could take it off, but
I'm scared.

Uncle Steve offered me his seat behind the bench, but I

couldn't take it. I don't want to cause a scene or distract Gabe during the last home game of the season. I know he's already heading to the playoffs and beyond that—the NFL.

Uncle Steve and Gabe are still tight. It's hard for me, but I'm happy for Gabe since his family is out of the picture.

I've seen him on campus a few times, but I always hung back not wanting to be seen.

I still love him with every breath I take, but when Mom chose to fight, we needed to band together and help. Dad stayed in Sea Spray to close out the season and Charlie started back in school.

Dad placed the key to the apartment by UVA in my hand, gave me a pat on the back and told me to pack up my room.

I did.

Sophie moved into the spare bedroom, and I'm finally living the college life. I've wanted to find Gabe a million times, but I can't. It'd be selfish when most of my time is spent at the library or hospital. The nurses give me weird smirks when I visit, too. Which is very strange—like they know some secret, I don't.

I got a spinal tap hoping I'd be the match for Mom, but I wasn't. Watching Charlie donate his was heartbreakingly beautiful. He's the bravest little boy, and one day he'll realize what he did for me. He saved our mother.

The stadium erupts as our QB Lincoln fakes a handoff and throws it long, right into Gabe's waiting hands. He sprints hard, evading tackles as he gets closer to the end zone.

Everyone is saying he's never played better. As soon as we know if Mom's transplant takes and she has her last treatment, I'll find him. His season should be over by then, and hopefully, it can just be us again.

He scores!

He takes his helmet off; arms pumping up the crowd.

He's happy.

Free.

Happier than I've ever seen. I understand him even better now; this sport makes him feel like he can do anything.

He makes me feel that way too. With a smile on my face, I slip from my seat, walk through the stands and out to my car.

I did the right thing letting him go—but I wouldn't bet on the game, just yet there's more time on the clock for us. Mom's out of the woods, for now, getting stronger every day, maybe just maybe—the time for me and Gabe to find our way back to each other will be sooner than I thought.

The leaves crunch under my boots, the air's chilly with the smell of fall. It's quiet as Soph, and I start the five-minute walk to Frat Row. Although I'm a pledge, I've managed to avoid most of the parties until tonight. The sisters have welcomed me with opened arms, even baking for my mom and the other patients on her floor.

The hospital staff loves our sorority. It's funny—I used to feel so alone, but now I'm part of an even larger family.

They all know about Gabe and me but don't ask. Since we've been broken up, I've been left alone. I feel like I can breathe again, focus on my life and family without the circus of the press interfering.

Gabe... he's still everywhere. His handsome face plastered on social media and the local news.

I can't escape him.

But I carry the memory of our love with me everywhere anyway.

"Are you sure there's a party tonight? This place is deserted." I jump at the unexpected sound of a hooting owl perched in a tree.

"Yes. There's no one home at the other frat and sorority houses because the fall bonfire is at ours. You'd know that if you listened to me while we were at the game instead of drooling at the sight of Gabe in his uniform."

"He did look good," I sigh.

"He did," she winks. "Who knows, maybe he'll be there tonight.

"Really?"

"Did you forget he's in Kappa Delta."

"We never talked much about it. I forgot."

"Have you spoken to him at all?"

"No. We've just exchanged a few texts here and there..."

"Hmmm...."

"What's that mean?"

"Nothing."

"Soph?" I grab her arm, spinning her around.

"I overheard some girls from another sorority during pledge week... one was bragging about hooking up with Gabe at a back to school mixer. She was probably just making it all up... "

"You don't look so convinced."

"She said... he was drunk and kept calling her 'Fanny...' she was brunette, like you."

"It doesn't sound like him. Gabe doesn't drink off-season. I can't picture him drinking during..."

"Like I said, I'm sure she was probably lying."

My smile's forced as we reach the end of the block where our sorority house is overflowing. People litter the lawn, the street; fireworks are going off out back.

"This party won't last long; the campus police won't let it."

"We have got a permit for the bonfire and fireworks... it's all been handled."

Despite the pit in my stomach, I follow Soph into the crowd.

"Pledges inside!" I've barely taken a sip from the warm beer I didn't want when my hand's grabbed. Someone puts me in a chicken wing, and a blindfold covers my eyes.

"What's going on?"

"Silence. Welcome to our watered-down version of hazing." A sharp voice answers. Unable to see, I'm led forward, told to climb a set of stairs and enter a dim room. My hands are freed, but I'm warned not to remove the blindfold.

"Pledges. Welcome to our fall bonfire. Each of you will enter Eden—our den of pleasure. You may strip, but you can't talk. Your safe word is red velvet. If you wish to consent to sex with one or more partners at the same time step forward now."

I'm frozen, in total shock the sorority I trusted—had a hidden dark side. But someone moves next to me—walking forward.

Silence follows.

"Well, we know which pledge is the dirty one! The joke is on Rachel... there is no den of pleasure! Rachel, you are on dish duty for the rest of the week. Will the remaining pledges take a step forward, please? The five of you will be escorted into the butler's pantry. This old colonial house has a small corridor with one door in and an opposite door out. You must leave your blinds on and meet with one of our frat brothers for five minutes. The boys have been warned—not to take more than a kiss or risk getting kicked out of the frat. This is meant to be for fun—not to make anyone feel uncomfortable."

I raise my hand, "I already feel uncomfortable."

"That's good, Callie. Since you've been picked to go first. The boys have been fighting over who gets to kiss you."

I open my mouth to protest, but it's too late. Strong hands

push me forward, I fall on the floor, hearing the click of a door shut and lock behind me.

"H-hello?"

There's silence, but I feel someone in the small hall with me.

Hands slide to the back of my head, through my long hair, then fingers trail over my cheek.

It has to be him.

His touch is something I'd never forget.

I stand on shaky legs, arms reaching out to grab hold of him to steady myself.

His hands roam down my back, my butt, and up around my stomach sliding over my breasts. He growls in the dark a second before his mouth crashes down on mine.

Knowing I have only minutes to sate months of pent-up hunger, my tongue dances with his. My thighs ache for him to come between them and my nipples peak dying for his kiss.

I cry into his mouth as his hand cups my breasts, his hips push me into the wall while his other hand picks up my legs to hook it around his waist.

"I should hate you for breaking my heart," he breathes a second before a piece of foil rips, and my jeans are jerked down my thighs.

"Tell me to stop. Tell me not to take you like an animal in a frat house with hundreds of people outside."

But I don't tell him to stop. Instead, I reach between us, stroking him through his jeans ripping the blindfold off at the same time.

"So, be it."

He takes his phone out, shooting off a text that he'll need ten more minutes with me. My eyes reading every word he types. I'm too needy for him to be embarrassed. Music starts pumping from somewhere beyond these four walls. My eyes close, head falls to the side as his mouth finds my neck at the same moment he slams inside.

"Fuck, Callie. You feel so good." He pumps into me over and over again; my ass is cradled in his hands as his hips pump into me again and again.

One hand falls, my legs are still wrapped around his lower back as he finds my clit with his finger, taking me over the edge.

"I love you," I moan, biting his shoulder.

"Be with me," he groans, emptying himself into the condom.

"I-I can't."

"Still running?"

His eyes are wounded as they search mine. "You know why. I'd drag you down and you—you haven't even begun to rise. I just know you're going to make it big, Gabe. I-I'm not cut out for that. I'm just a local girl from a beach town, with more sand than makeup on her face."

He shakes his head, fixes himself, and steps back.

"You're wrong. You were the girl who made me feel like she was all I needed. But if you can't be her—I'll need to find a way to live with it."

He turns away opening the opposite door. I sink to the floor, in a huddled mess, my body humming from pleasure and pain in the dark. I'm not sure how long I sit there stewing in regret, but the opening of the door behind me, has me blinking in the light.

All twenty of my sorority sisters stand with knowing grins on their faces until they see me sitting on the floor in the dark with tears streaming down my face.

"Did he hurt you?"

"No. I hurt him. Again."

"Why? This whole thing was a set-up. Gabe set all this up so that he could have five minutes in heaven with you. We all thought it was incredibly romantic." Angela, the Sorority President, stands confused staring at me like I'm the biggest idiot in the world.

"My mother's cancer is incredibly rare—so rare they think it might be hereditary, like a recessive gene or something. I'm scared. Scared to love anybody too much."

"Oh, Callie, why didn't you tell me?"

"Because, Soph, everyone already walks on eggshells around me. I didn't want that."

"You should tell him."

"No. He's playing the season he needs to reach the NFL. Telling him would only mess with his head." Angela shrugs, stepping forward to help me up.

"She's right. My brother's on a farm team for the Yankees. He's always telling us at the level he's at—stuff in his personal life is the only thing that can screw up his game more than an injury." Erin, another sister, speaks up for me.

"This is a pledge party, not a pity party. Let's help Callie get her groove on." I reluctantly follow them down the stairs, outside, leaving my tattered heart back on the closet floor.

My mind is full of him, as I sip a beer, standing on the outer circle by the fire. A few boys try to talk to me but give up when it's clear my mind is somewhere else.

"I'm getting a refill. Want one?"

I shake my head at Soph, freezing. On the other side of the fire, Gabe sits in a large deck chair, a brunette on his lap. She giggles, whispering into his ear. He looks up, sensing my stare.

Maybe the headlines held some truth after all. Twenty minutes after he took me like he'd die if he didn't; he's causally flirting with my look alike, relaxed with a beer in hand and I wonder if I ever really knew him at all?

THIRTY-SIX

CADE

I'm being a baby, pouting like a child that didn't get his way. But what else can I do? She doesn't want me, even when she does.

The beer I've been nursing is warm in my hand as I sit in the lawn chair, enjoying the view.

Callie has her back turned. My smirk grew bigger as each tool tried to make their move.

Gayle's doing better. I text her as much as Banger. But it's become too hard for me to visit her when I wish to be part of the family.

She understands, hoping just as much as I do—someday the time will be right.

"Hey, sexy." Fern Daniels straddles my hips. She's drunk as fuck. Her brother's on the hockey team, and we've hung out a few times in groups. She's not Callie, though, and we did nothing but share one disastrous kiss. It was a reminder that replacing one girl with another—would never work.

But I can't shove her off my lap.I'd better look out for her tonight. It's the right thing to do; her brother would kick my ass if one of these drunks got into her pants on my watch.

The hairs on the back of my neck rise.

Shit.

Callie's staring at me like she doesn't even see me.

Fern forgotten I jump up as Callie takes off. She runs through the yard, out to the street. Barely, jogging, I catch up.

"Callie? That wasn't what it looked like."

"It doesn't matter if it is. We're not together."

"We could be. I know everything. I can't keep pretending I don't."

"What do you mean?" She turns around with angry eyes reflecting moonlight.

"Your, mom. We stay in touch, daily." Taking out my phone, I scroll through dozens of texts.

"I can't believe the two of you. Treating me like a child? Plotting behind my back? Unbelievable."

Instead of holding me in relief, she walks away. "Stop chasing me, Gabe. Thank you for giving me a reason to finally help me get over this." She gestures between the two of us.

"How did it all go so wrong? We were so happy?" I call out.

"I don't know. It just did," she answers walking backward throwing her arms up.

I watched her walk away until the night swallowed her up, leaving me standing alone with my broken heart scattered across the road for all tires to roll over and crush some more.

I know I screwed up here, somewhere, but damn if I can figure out how or where.

THIRTY-SEVEN

I WALKED AWAY INTO THE DARKNESS leaving my heart behind. The truth was I am terrified to love him so much. I've been strong for everyone around me; Charlie, Dad, Mom... carefully hiding the fact that each day when I woke up pretending to be fine—I wasn't. Not even close. The weight of it all slowly chipped away at me.

Gabe, well, loving him not knowing where he could end up and knowing I can't leave to follow him, scared the shit out of me.

The pressure of the NFL, the fans, the fangirls, the crazies like his ex, can I cope with all that? Can he?

I toss on my bed, unable to sleep. The ceiling fan whirls above my head. I just broke my own heart tonight. Walking away from him was probably the stupidest thing I've ever done.

Throwing off the covers, I slip on a pair of jeans, grab my keys and cell. Walking carefully, not to wake Soph, I exit, locking the door behind me. I hop on my trusty bike and ride through deserted streets. The air is cold, but my legs push hard. It's about time I stop running from the one thing I truly want.

Thanks to Sop, I know where he lives.

It only took ten minutes to pedal over to the row of town-homes a few streets behind the football stadium. With a pounding heart and sweaty palms, I push down the kickstand and walk around to the back of his unit. Bending to pick up a few pebble in my hand, I take a deep breath. "Here goes nothing." The first small stone hits the glass before rolling down the roof.

Nothing.

I throw the second one. A small light switches on. A man's frame is silhouetted against the glass before it opens and a blonde haired, sexy beast of a man pops his head through, "wrong window, sweetheart."

"Banger?"

He grins, pointing a finger to the window next to his, "try that one."

"Can you just let me in?" I walk around to the front door and wait. Banger opens the door, standing shirtless with his hair tousled. He directs me to Gabe's room and I knock softly on the door. "It's me. I-I... we can't leave things the way we did. We deserve more."

"I completely agree."

He opens the door and towers above me. He's so strong and muscular. The perfect package—the perfect hero. And I hurt him. Badly When all he wanted to do is love me. After a few awkward seconds, he moves aside to let me in.

His room is neat and smells like home.

"Gabe...I-I love you. I love you so goddamn much it's too much."

"I know. Come here." His big arms embrace me.

We stand in the dark hugging one another. He kisses the top of my head and sighs deeply.

"I'd move the stars for you," He whispers.

"I know, because you already have. I just...there was so much going on with my mom and Charlie. My classes—the businesses. I was drowning. But you gave me so much, Gabe. This summer meant everything to me."

I pull back to cup his jaw. "I just don't want love to hurt anymore. You're going to go pro and I need to stay here with my mom and watch Charlie. I still have two years left and I still want to go to med school. That's always been my dream. But how can I chase that if I'm following you...watching you achieve yours?"

"I know baby," he sighs. " I just wish there was a way we could make it work. I already signed with an agent. I won't lie to you. I could get drafted this year and not finish here."

"Me too. But if we stay together, it'll only be harder when you go. It's going to break my heart wide open watching you go even though I'll be so happy for you. And I mean that. Watching you get everything you've worked so hard for, will bring me joy. But it will be bittersweet."

"Stay with me, Callie? One more night? I just want to hold you."

"I'd like that." I slip off my shoes and take his hand. He spoons me in his big bed and sighs into the dark, "I just know we belong together. Someday Callie. Someday, I'll come back for you. I swear it. I'm not done chasing you, babe."

I turn in his arms and kiss him while tears run down my cheeks. Soon our kisses become more urgent.

Hands slide and caress.

Soft sighs mingle in the dark.

Two hearts beat and break as one, hoping someday they'll be pieced back together.

He holds me into the dawn.

Then we both let go.

For now...

THIRTY-EIGHT

CALLIE

Two years later...

"IT'S GOING TO BE A HOT ONE a real scorcher." Banger comes on the morning show, stunning everyone at the café.

"Is that Banger? What's he doing at WFBN? I heard he replaced Seacrest at E."

Shrugging, I sit drinking my coffee, as I study the notes on my iPad. I might be home for the summer, but medical school is no joke. I graduated UVA a semester early since I doubled up attending the main campus all year and taking whatever credits I could here the past few summers. I never saw Gabe again after that night at the bonfire.

I told myself for years it was for the best, but every time I drive back to Sea Spray hitting the red light at the first intersection; my car idles as I reminiscence the night we first met.

"GOOOD MORNING SEA SPRAY! It's Banger coming to you live. I just couldn't stay away. I'm on vacation, visiting old haunts. The memories—they just come flooding back. My best ones are here in this town. But I'm not the only one taking a trip down memory lane—I'm live in studio with a very good friend..."

"Hey, Sea Spray... it's Parker. Some of you might remember me. Two years ago, this very weekend—I met the woman of my dreams right here. She slipped away, but I never forgot her. I see her face every time I close my eyes. She haunts my dreams, my heart, my soul... Fanny if you're out there—I still love you. I never stopped believing you'd come back to me. There's never been anyone else, I swear to you. If you still love me, too—meet me tonight. You know where."

My coffee cup slips from my hands.

I turn hot—cold—then hot again.

Gabe's here? He still loves me?

I've watched every game on TV, read every article written about him, but I never dared to hope he felt the same way since he never once tried to contact me after we broke up. I never got over him though. We tried so hard to make it work but everything changed. In order to pursue our dreams we had to let each other go, both of us swore that if we were meant to be we'd find our way back to each other.

I had planned to reach out to him and pour my heart out, but then the acceptance letter to Grad school in California came.

My mother told me to go—pursue my dreams and let Gabe chase his. She said sometimes we need to fulfill our own dreams or resent our partner if we don't. We watched the NFL draft together from the apartment. Both of us crying as he went in the third round to New England. Uncle Steve was there, with him in person, looking like the proud father figure he's become.

"You're going this time, right? I don't have to make a secret phone call? I never want to see Banger again, much less have to talk to him. But I'd do it for you."

"Will you finally, tell me what the heck happened between the two of you? Come on, Soph," I sigh. She wouldn't even tell me after eight Margaritas in Cabo on our graduation trip.

"Fine. If you promise to go. Remember pledge week? You weren't the only one suckered into going into a closet. Banger made them get me in one with him. We kind of hung out that summer, too. But he seemed like such a player that I wanted nothing to do with him. Especially since I had feelings for Elliott."

"What? You liked Elliott?"

"I did. But I'd never... you know because of you."

"Gabe always said Banger was a good guy. Maybe you should've given him a chance."

"Maybe. But that was years ago. He's famous now."

"So? So is Gabe."

"That's different."

"Is it? He might still be into you. It's probably hard to let people in because they might just want to be near you when you're famous."

"Don't forget, rich. You better go tonight."

"I'm going. I'm scared as hell, but I'm going."

"Call BC first. Get yourself transferred to med school in Boston."

"I did. Months ago, Baltimore is too gray, for me."

"Boston's not any better."

"But I'll have him."

"What are you waiting for? Go now!"

"I can't." I look down at my chipped nails and inspecting the ends of my hair. "I haven't had time to keep myself up. We never did take that spa day..."

THIRTY-NINE

GABE

I'm nervous as hell, but Gayle texted that she just left the house. She's become a second mother to me; it's been hard pretending otherwise since we've kept our communications quiet since Callie felt betrayed by it two years ago.

I never wanted Callie to feel pressured by my love. And I know if I went back for her two years ago—explained everything, starting with that afternoon I took her mother to the stadium; she would have given it all up for me. But Callie wouldn't have been happy as a trophy wife. I knew that. So, I kept my distance, each of us simultaneously pursuing our dreams on opposite coasts. But now the time is right. She's more confident than ever, pursuing her dream to be a physician and saving lives has given her this incredible confidence. Steve lets me stalk her Instagram and Facebook whenever we hang out. He laughs, that he'd charge me for stalking if I keep bugging him for more pics of her. He's texted more than a few over the years.

This time—I'm making my play and catching Callie for good.

She's there.

Sitting in the sand with her long hair whipping behind her. Her head turns at me walking up the beach at dusk.

"Hey. I'm Gabe Parker... in case you haven't heard of me— I'm kind of a big deal."

"I'm Callie, but the man I love calls me, Fanny."

I'm on her in an instant. Lips crushing hers, body pinning her down in the sand, like a wild beast.

"I'm sorry. I just—couldn't help it," I groan rolling to my side.

"Fuck it. I'm not sorry," she whispers moving to straddle me.

"I've missed you. So, fucking much."

"I've felt half-alive. Never, never leave me again."

"I won't. But technically—*you left me*. Twice."

"Shut up and kiss me."

So, I do and I never stop until we're both breathless and needy in the moonlight.

"We need to stop. There might be a dozen cameras on tripods somewhere out there." My head nods over to the ocean behind us.

"So? Let them take as many pictures as they can. I want the whole world to know we're back together."

I dip my head, pressing my forehead against hers, "God, Callie, you better mean that. I'm not letting you go this time."

"I do. I mean every word. I've missed you every day for years. I never stopped loving you, Gabe. Can you forgive me for chasing my dreams, too?"

"Ah, babe. There's nothing to forgive. I'm so proud of you. Imagine me, married to a doctor."

"Married?"

"We aren't headed anywhere but down an aisle."

"As long as you don't dress like Elvis and start serenading me with a cheesy love song."

"Admit, it. You missed my singing."

"I missed everything about you," she confesses cupping the side of my face.

Standing up, I reach down swinging her up in my arms carrying her down the beach.

"Gabe!" she squeals, throwing her hands around my neck as I swing her around in circles, "what are you doing?"

"Carrying you off down the beach, just like I fantasized about years ago."

"Do you mean that night at the Beachcomber?"

"Fuck, yeah. I'm going to do everything I wanted to you that night—tonight."

"Um, Charlie's home. He never stops talking about you."

"I miss him. But he'll have to wait until tomorrow. Tonight is all about you and me. Our reunion is going to be epic."

"Did you forget my parents are at the house, too?"

"Oh, we're not going to their house—we're going to ours."

Her beautiful brown eyes widen as I carry her up the beach and over the flagstone patio refusing to let her down until I've crossed the threshold of the beach cottage where we first fell in love.

"Gabe?"

"I bought it. It's ours, forever."

"Forever, sounds perfect."

I set her down, and she looks around. "It's exactly the same as I remembered."

"So are you," I breathe, reaching for her with shaking hands.

"What? Is my big, bad, pro player nervous to be alone with me?"

"Yes. I'm terrified. Terrified—I'm going to wake up and find out this was all a dream."

She slowly backs away from me, lifts her shirt over her head, tossing it, "catch."

I snag it with one hand. "You don't want to talk first? Catch up on what our lives have been like?"

She answers by unsnapping her bra, letting it dangle from a finger. "It's called pillow talk, Gabe."

"Oh yeah? Who have you been having that with?" I growl, stalking her as she walks up the stairs backward.

"You. I laid awake in the dark, talking to the ghost of you."

I cut the distance between us in three giant steps. "I'm right here, Callie. I always was. I always will be."

Using our hands and mouths, instead of words—we cling to each other deep into the night, pressed skin to skin, high on the feeling of being reunited after so long.

I wasn't joking about marrying her. It's what I always envisioned for us, ever since that summer two years ago where I caught her, and she ended up stealing my heart.

EPILOGUE

GABE PARKER FINALLY GETS HIS BRIDE
By Jen Krug

Former UVA football star and local
    heartthrob Gabe Parker married
    his mystery girl last week in Martinique.
    Parker plays for the Patriots
    where last season he led them
    to yet another Super Bowl win. His
    wife, Callie Anderson, is our favorite
    local girl now lead trauma surgeon
    at Brigham and Young hospital in
    Boston. You might remember how
    the glamorous couple met right here
    in Sea Spray five years ago, amid the
    University cheating scandal in which
    Parker was later found to be innocent.
    He was cleared but never

out of the press as his ex at the
time was charged with kidnapping
Anderson's brother. Parker made
plenty of waves here in Sea Spray, and
many won't forget that sunny summer
morning where across the radio
waves; he declared his love for his
mystery girl. They dated for a brief
period, somehow he fumbled, but later
reclaimed his love once again calling
out over WFNB's morning show.
The couple resides in Marble Head,
Massachusetts with their pet iguana
Butch and a few house cats. It is rumored
that Parker was offered Dancing
with the Stars but turned it down
since it films in LA, away from his
new leading lady. A few guests have
revealed that he serenaded his bride,
singing, "Make You Feel My Love"
while a teary crowd looked on.

Former Sea Spray DJ wins Emmy for musical score in new Danny G film.
By Birdie Hun

Banger. No one knows where he came from, but Sea Spray has
never been the same since he left. The former morning show
host at WBFN and resident DJ at Beachcomber's the last
decade is now taking Hollywood by storm. Banger is the new
face of E television with several movies in the works.

Our former resident bad boy might be off the market, rumor has it he was seen canoodling with another Sea Spray local gal, Sophie Merchant.

Must be something in the water!

Our local girls are catching big fish!

Ruthless.
Dangerous.
Royal.

WOLF of WASHINGTON

CLAIRE WOODS

MORE FROM CLAIRE

Coming Winter 2021

WOLF OF WASHINGTON

THEY CALL HIM "THE WOLF."

When I danced with him at the New Year's Eve ball, I sensed the danger in him. It lurked right below the surface of his Armani tuxedo. But when he held me in his arms; his touch was gentle fire, snaking along my skin.

I was attracted to it. To him.

His grey eyes burned as they lazily traveled over my form-fitting gown and naked arms. I sensed his hunger as he peered through his mask, down to the swell of my breasts.

"Dance with me." He commanded.

I was playing Cinderella, and *it was a ball*. The most exclusive New Year's Eve ball in the world; invite only, where the elite mixed amongst themselves, parading behind masks and clothes suited for royalty—in the Golden Age.

My best friend Sasha found herself unexpectedly swept off

her feet by a pro rugby player she met doing a swimsuit shoot in Australia.

It was strictly prohibited; against the rules—to pass on your invite, but she was always a rule-breaker while I was the straight-laced one.

But just for one night—I wanted to be the rule-breaker.

He pressed me closer to his chest, his erection firmly nestling between my thighs as we swayed to the music

It felt divine to be wanted—craved by a man like him.

He held me in his arms, murmuring sweet words into my hair in a language I didn't understand. They wove around me like a spell; seducing me. I pressed closer against him, and he growled low in his throat.

The wolf wanted his woman and that woman was me.

He danced me over to the glass doors without me even realizing, sweeping me outside and into the moonlight.

"A full moon on New Year's Eve?" I murmured in wonder.

His teeth nipped my ear as he stood behind, keeping me warm in his tight embrace.

"What's your name?" I had asked... for the third time. And like the other times I had asked, he didn't answer.

He turned me in his arms, claiming my mouth like Troy claimed Helen. But I don't have a face that would launch a thousand ships. But he couldn't guess whose face was under the delicate mask made of silk and beads that shimmered in the light. Only my best feature showed; green eyes framed by lashes so long I often get accused of wearing a false set.

I felt like an imposter; a fraud.

I'm an ordinary woman cloaked in an amazing gown. And thanks to Jenny Craig and CrossFit—it fit me like I was born in it.

His mouth moved over mine, urgently deepening our kiss.

"Wolf." He turned. For the first time, I noticed the men standing guard in the shadows.

"What?" he rasped.

"He's on the phone." He tightened his hold on me before letting go.

"Stay here." He demanded, ripping off his mask. He was talking so intently on the cell his man had given him, that he didn't notice my gasp or see me slowly inching to the stairs leading from the balcony to the wooded garden below. My prince charming was a beast, the most ruthless man in D.C.—maybe even the world. His face was all hard lines and sculpted bones, bred from generations of royals only breeding with the best in the gene pool.

He was magnificent. Terrifying. I fled like little red riding hood, desperate to escape before he took everything from me.

I was gone, running through the branches full of sparkling lights, fumbling in my purse for the valet ticket. His roar was so loud not even the ringing bells and cheers of midnight could drown it. Pounding footsteps and the shouts of his men quickly followed.

The wolf was stalking his prey.

But he was to be denied.

I got away, barely. Of all the things, it was a cocktail waitress who saved me. I yanked her by the arm, begged her to trade places as I raced inside a side door and into a coat room. She was worried about her tips until I grabbed a few hundred dollars in change and shoved them in her hands. Five minutes later, she was still struggling to get the zipper of the gown to go all the way up as I slipped out of the room with my ticket in hand.

Guards with radios flanked every exit. But I passed by unnoticed. For they were looking for the great beauty, cloaked in an equally beautiful golden gown, not a serving wench with a baggy uniform and a hanging head.

I handed the valet my ticket, and he arched a brow. "What? I punched out early." I had challenged. He finally left to fetch my car.

The hairs on the back of my neck rose, the wolf was ten feet behind me, questioning why the best guards on the continent hadn't found me yet.

They assured him it was just a matter of time. Voices shouted with triumph. I had been spotted. I was about to be secured. He raced up the stairs, taking them two at a time, at the same time my Volvo stopped at the curb. I looked back one last time. He was on the second-floor balcony, holding his head in apparent agony when they brought the imposter to him. I pushed the doors open, jumped into my car and hit the gas.

My eyes flicked to the rearview mirror, half expecting a fleet of dark cars giving chase.

But I had escaped the most dangerous man in town. Thank God, he had taken off his mask. I was drunk on his scent, pulled under by his masculinity and almost did something stupid. I would've gone blindly, right into his lair. And I know with certainty once he found out who I was one of two things would've happened. He'd tie me to his bed: making me his personal sex slave, or leave me in a dungeon, holding me captive while demanding answers.

He's the ruthless "Wolf of Washington, but I'm just an average woman; the plain Jane who ran away from him.

But I still had one night.

I danced, kissed and was held by him, *for one night.*

It's with resolute certainty, I know without a doubt—his eyes will haunt my dreams for the rest of my life.

Year after year will go by, and as the clock ticks down to

midnight on New Year's Eve—I'll remember the magic of the one I danced in his arms until the magic of time turns to dust.

Wolf

I still smell her on me. Her taste is still in my mouth.

I hunger for her.

Thirst for her kiss.

"Dammit." The glass of Scotch that was in my hands hurls across the room smashing against the brick wall of the fireplace. Flames shoot outwards as the alcohol burns. Shards of glass glitter like the diamond in my hand.

It's the most brilliant one I've mined. I'm keeping it for the one woman who will rule my heart... *hell rule my world.*

I've never been the one to bed a thousand women, then leave discarding them like trash.

No. I always craved my mate. I'd cherish her. Keep her close—kill anyone who tried to take her from me.

My fists clenches so hard, the rough-cut stone slices my palm as I walk to the floor to ceiling window and peer out into the city below. The flags from embassy row, ripple in the wind, the dome of the Capital building rising like a full moon behind. I take my cigar out and lit it. Closing my eyes, I inhale deeply seeing her standing in the crowd. Even with her face hidden, she stood out from all the rest.

She was the fair maiden at a ball in the fairy tale. *My fairy tale.* And dammit I want my happy ending with a bride in my bed.

I'm forty-two. I need an heir. But something felt missing with every woman I've dated. There was no spark. No heat. No longing to take them in my arms and never let go.

She's out there. *I will find her.*

Unlocking the balcony doors, I step out and grip the icy, wrought iron railing. The cold burns just as much as the heat.

Two hours, twenty-five minutes and ten seconds. That's how long it's been since I held her in my arms. My face nuzzled her hair. My tongue dueled with hers.

I had her.

She was mine.

Until my mask came off. She saw who I was. Who I am. The wolf. Ruthless hunter. Royal Ambassador by day and diamond trader by night. Although dealing in diamonds in only half true. It's a front. A façade to conceal what I'm really after... finding the arm's dealer supplying the pirates off the Somali Coast. The one's responsible for killing my parents, leaving me alone in the cold world of aristocracy.

After they died, my cousins Andreas and Matteo become my brothers. I'd kill or die for either one of them and they would do the same for me.

"Wolf. We tracked down the hidden code printed on the back of the invitation to the ball... it was Sasha Bennet's."

"It wasn't her. I've met her before. She was unremarkable."

"Only you, would find a world-renown supermodel unremarkable," Andreas snorts.

"Well cousin, you know I have eclectic tastes."

"Sasha's in Australia. Should I get the gulf stream ready?"

"No. My woman is here. She's hiding right under my nose. Not a half a world away. Did you get her number?"

"I did."

I snuff out my cigar and hold out a hand. He places the slip of paper in it and I waste no time taking out my phone and tapping the digits in.

"H-hello?" She answers breathlessly.

"Where is she... who is she?" I demand.

"Who is this?"

"You know who this is," I growl in response.

"Wolf?"

"Ah, so she told you who held and kissed her all night... why did she run Sasha?"

I hear her sharp intake of breath and wait... I hold my phone out in disbelief. She hung up on me. She dared to hang up on... me?

"Call the pilot and fire up the jet. You're going to the land down under. Get answers for me Andreas. Tie her up if you need to."

He raises an eyebrow, "This woman really did something to you, didn't she?"

I turn back to the city below my feet, bury a fist in a pocket and bow my head, "She did."

"What if you find her and it's all for nothing? She could be married... a shrew—hell she could be ugly as hell. You never even saw her face, Marco."

"I didn't need to. Not when I felt her soul. When I held her in my arms, her touch burned me like a brand. I will find her."

"I have no doubt that you will. I just hope she's everything you think she is... for your sake. And if I have to kidnap Sasha Bennett to help you... well that's going to be a *delight*, for sure."

AFTERWORD

Thank you for reading Gabe and Callie's story! If you love them as much as I do—please leave a review! They help new authors like me so very much!

http://bit.ly/CatchingCallie

Follow me on BookBub or Facebook to make sure you don't miss Wolf's release or my next Holiday Romance!
Claire

Or
Join my mailing list for giveaways, join my ARC or BETA team and keep in touch!

BookBub: http://bit.ly/2NacQc0
FACEBOOK: http://bit.ly/AuthorClaireWoods

CPSIA information can be obtained
at www.ICGtesting.com
Printed in the USA
BVHW031301201221
624516BV00004B/86

9 781717 713520